A CONFERENCE OF VICTIMS

A

Conference

OF

Victims

◆ A NOVEL ◆

Gina
Berriault

COUNTERPOINT
BERKELEY, CALIFORNIA

A CONFERENCE OF VICTIMS

Library of Congress Cataloging-in-Publication Data
Names: Berriault, Gina, 1926- author.
Title: A conference of victims : a novel / Gina Berriault.
Description: Berkeley : Counterpoint, 2023. | "Earlier versions of this novel were published under the title Conference of victims, in 1962 by Atheneum and in 1985 by North Point Press."
Identifiers: LCCN 2022056922 | ISBN 9781640095960 (paperback) | ISBN 9781640096028 (ebook)
Subjects: LCSH: Suicide victims—Fiction.
Classification: LCC PS3552.E738 C59 2023 | DDC 813/.54—dc23
LC record available at https://lccn.loc.gov/2022056922

Cover design by Lexi Earle
Book design by Laura Berry

COUNTERPOINT
2560 Ninth Street, Suite 318
Berkeley, CA 94710
www.counterpointpress.com

Printed in the United States of America

1 3 5 7 9 10 8 6 4 2

We are created from and with the world
To suffer with and from it day by day:
Whether we meet in a majestic world
Of solid measurements or a dream world
Of swans and gold, we are required to love
All homeless objects that require a world.

—W. H. AUDEN, *Canzone*

A CONFERENCE OF VICTIMS

I

The day was election day but Hal O. Costigan, candidate for Congress, was nowhere around to have his picture taken as the winner or the loser. By his own choice he was nowhere around to care. The day was warm and windless, the large flags at the polling places rustling a little toward evening. Inside garages swept clean and living rooms tidied up, women with an official look appropriate to the day sat at card tables and checked off the names of the voters. Everything was as it should be, except one: a dead man's name was on the ballot.

Naomi Costigan did not vote. Her brother was dead and she had no use for all the other men whose names were on the ballot. Whatever they had promised to do meant nothing to her. She went to work at the county recorder's office and was deaf to the prophetic voices in the portable radios that some men carried with them to the counter and along the courthouse corridors. The only thing she heard that day was what she expected to hear that night, her mother's grief over the loss of the son.

They sat at the kitchen table facing each other, the bereft mother and her forty-year-old daughter, dipping their spoons into their bowls of soup. The mother wore her son Hal's high school cardigan sweater, its emerald green dulled by the years but the emblem still secure above a pocket. Maybe old women should never comb their hair, Naomi thought. They look worse when their hair is parted and smoothed down, like children keeping themselves neat so life will love them.

"Cort," said her mother, "I told Cort, 'You're his brother. It's your duty to find out who killed him. That's why a mother has more than one son, so they'll protect each other. If one is murdered, the brother never rests until he finds out who did it.' But Cort's a coward. He's got a birthmark on his back looks like a little eel."

"It always looked like nothing to me," said Naomi.

"An eel. He was always slippery."

Naomi did not defend her younger brother. Their mother loved him and that was his defense.

"Isobel," said her mother, "I said to her, 'Isobel, you're his wife. You go to the mayor, you tell him they killed Hal. The man he was running against got the police to do it.' The mayor would have listened to her, but she ran away. First she sent the boy off on a plane, alone, and then she runs away herself."

Elbows on the table, the mother crumpled the

pink paper napkin under her cheekbone, into the sagging flesh, and Naomi thought, betrayingly, that she had never seen a face so intricately wrinkled, like a puzzle God presented to the daughter's gaze for her to figure out, like a warning to the daughter to act, to run, before it was too late. But how could you escape if love and conscience were your jailers?

"Can you imagine her sending him off like that? A little boy? On the plane alone. Suppose her aunt, who was going to meet him, didn't get there, something happened, and there he'd be, alone. Any degenerate could of got hold of him. They walk around everywhere, and whores, the lowest of the low."

"I walk around, too," said Naomi, and saw that her mother couldn't tell whether the daughter was lowering herself to belong among the lowest or elevating herself to belong among the virtuous ones who were also present in the world.

"Why didn't they ask that girl if *she* murdered him? They hired a little whore to do it. They hired a little whore to say he slept with her."

"Mama, cut it out."

"They didn't find any note because the girl did it. No note."

"No note!" Naomi gripped the table edge. "Mama! He didn't need to leave a note. He said it loud, Mama, like they told him to speak up in debating class. He told us everything just by what he did to himself."

"What's everything?"

"Mama, I don't know what it is. How can *I* know?"

How could his dimwit, homely, job-bound sister, Naomi, know what *everything* was? If she lived to be a hundred, she'd never know.

Naomi shook out a cigarette from the package by her plate. "Who's President?" she asked brightly. "Eisenhower, I bet."

"Hal would of won," her mother said.

"Oh, he had it in the palm of his hand." Was it something called privilege her brother had, right from the day of his birth, and thrown away? Maybe she, too, Naomi, had been granted a privilege of sorts. Maybe you had to think so in order to live, and what was hers? A long time ago she had got herself a job, in the time of the jobless when sad-eyed men came to the back door to ask if they could earn a bite to eat. She had begun to support her mother and her brothers, and was that her privilege? That must have been it, and, though times had changed, forever after she had clung to it, that astounding privilege, as if it were her very life.

The unlit cigarette on her lip, she leaned to the radio on the counter, twirling the dial from music to audience laughter. A comedian's voice, falsely modest, falsely hesitant, insinuated its way into the expectant laughter and capped the joke. Louder laughter and the crackle of applause tumbled out into the kitchen.

"It's your friend," Naomi said. "The Great Goofball. He should've run for President. I would've voted for him."

The announcer's voice cut into the laughter and applause, switching the listeners, Naomi and her mother among them, to cities where counting was in progress, the microphone moving westward from New York to Chicago to San Francisco, the nearest large city to their own small city in the interior of the state. Excited voices rattled off the names of the candidates and the number of votes for each, so far, but the name of Hal Costigan was never spoken, as if the name had never appeared on a ballot or the man had never appeared on earth.

2

On the front page of the evening newspaper her father brought home, there was a photo of her under the headline COSTIGAN KILLS SELF OVER SCHOOL-GIRL. That morning when she had left the sheriff's office, her father had tried to put his jacket around her, but, alarmed by this closing-in from behind her of a garment that wasn't hers, she had thrust it away, and the camera caught her with her elbow lifted in a way that twisted her body and exaggerated her breasts in the cotton dress. *Dolores Lenci, 17-year-old paramour,* the caption said. She had never seen that word before.

They had come to the house in the morning, after a farmer's children, going down their dirt road to the highway to catch the school bus, had come upon his car parked among the willows. They knew, the sheriff's deputies, that she had been the last person with him that night. They knew because a deputy, cruising the outskirts of the city and surprising lovers in cars parked off country roads, had surprised them, had contemptuously asked her her name and her age, and contemptuously not asked the name of the man with her because he was recognizable in the flashlight as the young, respectable attorney, father, husband, and candidate for U.S. Congress. In the sheriff's office they had questioned her about what he had said that night, whether he had told her anything about the campaign, about money, about enemies, whether he had threatened to kill himself, whether her father had threatened to kill him, whether she had threatened, and though they asked their questions as if they knew what they were after, she felt that they were asking for no answer, only enjoying themselves, titillating themselves with the presence of the girl whose lips could barely move.

Dolores's mother came in after the cafe was closed and sat down on the bed, but the girl pushed away the hand that was dear to her and covered her face again with the blanket. Whenever her mother came to her, that evening and again in the morning, her mother was the stranger, her hand was not *his* hand and could not go to the parts of her body where his had gone; but in the hours she was alone, *he* was the stranger. Her body bore the impress of the stranger. At times his strangeness, intensified by his act of suicide—who was he?—bore down upon her and, with hands, with mouth, with whispers, set all the places astir again, each place desiring, until all was clamor. By his dying he had made the demand upon her to *know* him.

At noon, the next day, alone in the house, she sat at the kitchen table and read the two days of newspapers and gazed at the photographs of him, Hal Costigan, and his wife and his son and even his sister, who stared at the camera from among the record books and filing cabinets in the county recorder's office. She gazed at herself on the front page and saw nothing in that girl to warrant the man's risking anything for, and the thought that he might already have known what he would do if they were caught and had risked his life for her—that thought was a burden. She fed herself tasteless toast and wept, not for him and not for herself, but in fear of all the things she knew nothing about, until the newspaper pictures between her elbows grew damp and dark and the type showed through from the page underneath.

"What did he do it for?" She asked it of her father as he was taking off his shoes in the kitchen.

"What you got to learn," he said, pulling at a dusty boot, "is that everybody is a little bit crazy."

He glanced at her sideways, a secret glance of satisfaction that said the most respected, the most popular, the ones on their way up, as Costigan, were no better than the dolts, than himself, a maintenance man in an oil refinery, and, in this glance that was without any sympathy for the dead man, he revealed a stoniness of heart she had not glimpsed before. It was not that way all the time, his heart. Only now, and was it his own little bit of craziness? She opened a can of beer for him and set it on the table with a glass, and when he glanced up, his fatherly love for her had returned to his eyes.

After a week she went back to school. She told herself not to keep her eyes down, but they went down anyway, there were so many eyes looking at her. She had always met the eyes of the men who came into her mother's cafe because it was her way of telling them that she was somebody else beside the girl they were appraising. She was somebody who could appraise them, but always in this exchange was the excitement, concealed or unconcealable, of joining in the discovery of herself. Now she was unable to return anyone's gaze because the discovery of herself was public knowledge. A man had died and told them all about her. She wore a buttoned sweater that was too large and a bulky pleated skirt, but under these garments was the girl who had lain with the man.

When she came into the cafeteria, the voices went silent, the clatter dimmed down. When she went along the halls from class to class, clusters of boys would fall silent and watch her walk by, the more nervous among them laughing. The girls in the lavatories stopped their chattering or their languid conversations, and she did not look at herself in the mirror or stay long enough to comb her hair. The teachers were as respectful of her as though she had lain sick for a month, but they were self-conscious before their students, and all lectures and all formulae pointed to on the blackboard seemed as trivial to the teachers as they were to the students.

In the home economics class where, a month ago, the teacher had singled her out as an example of a "neat-minded" girl, she sat in her commendable style and embarrassed the teacher by confronting her with her teacher's superficiality, for within the nice clothes was the body that was not, and within the candidate's suit from the best men's store in the city, behind the smile, the wit, the eloquence, the respectability, everything that had charmed the teacher, was the man who had lain with the girl.

The newspaper photos of the funeral troubled her, in the days after. The women in black, a color incriminating of her, had known him better than she had known him, and they mourned the man they knew, while she went around the house in her pastel cotton dresses or in her sky-blue bathrobe. The figures in black accused her of ignorance of him and of destroying him, and she could not turn the blame on him because his suicide seemed to be an act of expiation. The girl with her long brown hair, which she had let grow long because it was exciting to men to see it hanging down her back, the girl alive and aware of her tantalizing self, *she* was to blame. She accepted the blame because the mystery of her lifted her above the sordid and, after a time, above the blame, and, without blame, she called up the times on the blanket in the back of the station wagon parked among the yellow willows by the creek. She became the girl desired beyond any risk, and the memory of herself and the man overcame her as she sat in study hall, her head bowed over a book, as she walked home, as she lay in her bed at night. All the details of love, the entwining of bodies, everything was recalled, and the time she had drawn herself upon him and loosened her hair into a dark silken enclosure for their faces and in that enclosure drawn upon his mouth until, with a sudden knotting of his body, he had thrust her under him. Again the willow branches scratched the windows, stirred by the night wind that moved like a creek above the creek; again the yellow-smoke trees surrounded them as she lay in the blanket he had wrapped her in to cover her nakedness, which he had explored and still explored; and again she lifted her head from his chest because his heart was beating under her ear—an overwhelmingly secret sound, the heartbeat of a stranger.

On election day her father came home early, bringing another worker from the refinery. They had been given an hour off at the end of the day and had gone to vote, and they sat in the kitchen, making jokes about the election. She was peeling potatoes at the sink, carefully so the peeler wouldn't nick the pink polish on her fingernails, aware of her long back and broad hips in the schoolgirl skirt and sweater and of the man's shy curiosity about her, notorious daughter of his co-worker.

"What the hell anybody want a change for?" her father asked his friend. One foot was up on a chair, and he lifted his foot to give the chair a push with it. "It's always the same bullshit, both sides the same bullshit, and when they get in themselves, where's the change?"

"There's a difference," the friend said, his arms leisurely on the table. "With the Democrats you get war, and with the Republicans you get a depression."

She had heard conversations like this before and they had meant little to her, but now she felt a rising resistance, an alarm that she tried to stop with the deadening sound of her hair falling across her ears as she bent her head lower. They recalled government scandals, bribery, and every name they spoke and every acquittal and conviction deprived her of her mystery, brought her down into the arms of a petty politician who had gone berserk with the idea that everything was due him, with wanting everything.

3

As Cort Costigan prepared himself to meet his girl, as he showered, shaved, brushed his teeth, shined his shoes, and then resented his being forced to make himself as handsome and as clean as possible when, after all, he was a plain fellow not always scrupulously clean, as he fretted over his falsified self but was pleased by the sight of himself at his best, he was preparing also the revelation of his inward self. He was not preparing the revelation in words because he was afraid of words. Words had a life of their own beyond him. Once when the words *great guy, oh, he was a great guy* spoke themselves inside his ears, startling him, he clamped his hands down over his head in a desperate stifling reflected in his bathroom mirror.

Pauline was already at the door when he drove up to her sister's house, already down the stairs and opening the car door, and was already sitting close to him before he was ready for the transition from the woman of his fantasies to the solid woman animated not by his wishes but by her own, a tall, big-boned, large-breasted girl with a sullen, bony face and straight blond hair to her shoulders. She sat against him, her skirt flaring over his knee, dispelling with her closeness the two days since he had seen her last and in which time his need for her had struggled with his doubts about his need. When she sat by him, he needed her, and this need increased through the evening along with his need to unburden himself of his brother. Now that he had found this girl, it seemed to him that he had been searching for her ever since his brother died, through the winter and into the summer, but he was reluctant to admit to himself his desire to exploit the tragedy of his brother for the benefits he hoped to get from it, the comforting and the passion that he hoped the story would arouse in her.

After the movie, they wandered around the library grounds, over grass illumined by the neon signs of the theater and the bar across the street, pausing to embrace in the shadows under the trees. It was a warm night in the middle of summer. They circled the old, cream-colored, two-story library, its high stone steps lit by a large white globe on each side, and found a bench at the back, under the windows of the basement reading room. They watched other couples crossing the grounds to their cars slowly, as if wading through the short grass, heard their voices carrying far in the quiet night, heard car doors slam and motors start, and a wakened bird complaining among the thick branches above their heads. Then he heard the words begin, as adroitly fumbled as if he had permitted himself to rehearse them that way.

"Pauline, Pauline, I want to tell you about my brother . . . ," and the use of his grief to persuade her to love him deepened his grief. "He was a great guy, a great guy."

"I know he was, Cort."

"No, I'm not saying it like in the obituary. That's not what I'm saying."

"I know what you're saying," she told him, stretching her fingers between his fingers.

"No you don't. You can't know until I tell you because I'm the one it happened to. I mean, my mother and Naomi, they cried and they still cry, my mother does, but it didn't shake them. My mother cries and goes right on watching television, and Naomi goes to work and goes home and talks about nothing and eats half a berry pie and drinks twelve cups of coffee up to the time she goes to bed. I don't drop by much anymore. That's the way women are, they survive. The men get killed in a war and the women put ashes on their heads and fight over the men who come back. Mama and Naomi, they got each other. But *me*," he said. "It did me in."

"It didn't do you in." She was stroking his sleeve. "You got a job, you got me, you laughed so hard tonight, the time the guy was holding onto the balloon."

"You ever look up to anybody? I looked up to him like he was my father. He was nine years older than me, and my father died when I was four, so it was easy for me to look up to him. I learned from him. He was my brother and my father, he was the man in the family. You know what I thought when I heard he was dead? I thought—somebody did it to him. All these years he's been showing me how to live. But after a while I had to admit he did it to himself. I had to admit it. I had to admit you don't do something like that to yourself without saying it's the thing to do. Jesus Christ, why did he tell me that?"

A man, standing on the curb before the bar, way across the grounds, glanced toward them, hearing Cort's faraway voice rising.

"You've heard the old saw about the good die young? It's true, they're killed off in the scramble to get to the top. What I mean, they're stepped on because they can't step on anybody because they don't like the goddamn war that goes on all the time. Or they do themselves in like my brother did. I look around me, I look at the other salesmen, and I think to myself—Jesus Christ, is that what we're put on this earth for, to sell goddamn refrigerators, hop-skip up to a customer before the other guy gets to him, make a big production out of a bloated piece of tin with an electric wire coming out of it?"

She was scratching his scalp with her long, strong fingers, her pointed fingernails. "But everybody said it was the girl," her voice low, curious.

"You sound like my mother, you sound like Naomi. Naomi asked me, 'You ever seen her, Cort?'" imitating his sister's grainy, whispery voice. "Mama wanted me to go over there and shoot her, she had this crazy idea about me avenging my brother, maybe something she picked up from a soap opera. If the girl was the reason, he made her the reason on purpose. He wasn't a kid, he didn't get all worked up like a kid does, you know how it was in high school, can't eat, can't sleep, can't live if you can't have the girl. Once he took me in there, bought me lunch there at her mother's joint, and she was there. It was a couple months before. She was there, it was Saturday, and he treated her like he treated any other waitress, considerate, kind of indifferent, too. I don't think he knew her name. She was just like any other good-looking high school girl, tall, long hair in a pony tail, used her hips like they do. You see them all the time, everywhere. But he said something to me I remember, he said something out of the Bible. He said, 'King David was old and stricken in years and his servants covered him with robes, but the old man was still cold. So his servants found a fair young virgin for him, and she ministered to him and lay down on his breast.' He quoted the Bible word for word, he was always good at that, and he said, 'That's an idea, isn't it? Bring in a young girl to warm up an old man in his last days. That's what I need.' And I said, 'You aren't old.' And he said, 'They call me young. Young Costigan. The young can act, the young can change things, there's nothing the young can't do, it takes a young man for the job. But I'm not young, I'm nine hundred and sixty-seven years and I'm cold. They cover me with campaign posters, I got this nice English suit, I got wool blankets and my wife Isobel and my son and life insurance, I got all that to keep me warm. But how does the Bible say it? He 'gat no heat?'" The tenor ring of his brother's voice—he heard it again, and he remembered that his brother had laughed, shifting in his seat in the booth, so unaware of the girl that if he were to choose some handmaiden she would not be the one.

Pauline was comforting him, stroking his shirt, un-buttoning one button to slip her hand inside and stroke his chest, and he drew her face to his, a swift claim-ing of her. "Come home with me," he begged her. "You want to come home with me, don't you?"

When he returned alone to his apartment and lay down alone where both had lain, the sorrow he had made use of to bring her to his bed, and that she had soothed away with her embrace, reclaimed him. Pauline's embrace, her long, strong arms and legs around him, had claimed him for only part of the night. As he was falling asleep, he was wakened by a clear convincing of his own self with the story he had told her. His brother had tried to link himself with life, one last attempt, just as the old king had tried, but the cold was already in the marrow of his bones. But *himself*? Cort Costigan? The younger brother wanted to live more than he wanted to die, and the girl who had embraced him an hour ago had more power over death than the girl who had lain in his brother's arms, and he drew her back again, Pauline, young woman fragrant with life, odorous with life.

4

Naomi, following her friend Athena into the bar's blue-glass entry, was reminded of a black-fig tree on a summer day, of the smell of the figs fallen to the ground and beaten to a fermenting pulp by the hot sun. The summers of her childhood were surprisingly contained in this unfamiliar bar one step from the cold street of late October.

"Smells like old figs. You know, old fruit," she said, tittering, stumbling because it was so dark inside, only the mirror behind the row of bottles lit by an amber light.

"That's everybody's breath you smell," Athena said, the lifting of her voice like a greeting to the bartender. "They never air the place. Everybody's old whisky breath stays in here."

"Some people need it like oxygen," said the bartender, a tall old man, bald. He was turned to the mirror, fussing with something, and Naomi saw his face and the back of his head at the same time. The double image heightened her wariness.

Athena dropped her purse on the small round table and pulled out a spindly chair. Naomi, in imitation, pulled out the other spindly chair and sat down. Her knees, as she crossed them, kicked up the table and joggled the amber glass ashtray.

"It's so damn dark in here," Athena said, explaining away Naomi's clumsiness. "Over at the Executive they got two sixty-watts going day and night."

"They can afford it," said the bartender.

A young man at the end of the bar turned his face toward them, taking them in and disgorging them at the same time. "That's where the bigshots hang out," he said. "The D.A., the mayor, those guys. Every time I go in there I see big money passed under the table."

"You're crazy, boy," the bartender said. "They do that kind of thing in privacy." He lifted his eyebrows at the women. "What'll it be?"

"A martini for me," Athena said.

"Privacy!" The young man blew his lips out to make an obscene noise. "Who's private? Everybody writes their mem-wahs about who they screwed, all the movie stars write their mem-wahs. Big swindlers, big gamblers, they all write their mem-wahs. Privacy ain't natural."

"He sounds like my dad," Athena said, bowing her shoulders with a secret laugh.

"Sounds like Mama," Naomi said, and she too bowed, laughing.

The bartender, deaf to the young man at the bar, was tipping his head toward Naomi, his eyebrows still lifted queryingly.

"Oh, it'll be the same for me," Naomi said. She was familiar with martinis. Her brother Hal had taken her into the Executive a few times and she had liked martinis best, and this possession of a preference made her feel at home now.

"My old dad hates everybody," Athena said. "I got it figured out that the closer you get to dying, see, the closer you get to being alone the rest of eternity, the more you want to be alone. It's kind of like nature preparing you."

"My mother's not that bad," Naomi said. "She's got pity for orphans. One time there was a piece in the paper about five kids left in a room by their mother. She went out with some guy and there they were with no food, no fire, nothing, and one kid real sick."

Athena shrugged off her coat with a nervous, coquettish movement that went from her shoulders down her arms to her dry, wrinkled hands and their nails heavy with red polish. "There was this father who was shot by his boy scout son. You remember, up in Lassen County? My dad says, 'Must of been a mean bastard, guess he deserved it.' Then he says, 'Boy must be crazy, whole family crazy.' Course me," she said, twisting her red beads, "I feel sorry for the father, you know, but I feel even worse for the boy. There in one minute his whole life is ruined. The father, he lived his life and maybe he didn't live it right and maybe he shouldn't of brought kids into the world. Or maybe he lived it right, they say he was a church elder. Who knows? You never know what goes on inside a house. But I feel sorrier for the boy. You think, someday he'll wake up and realize what he did, and then you think, he's never going to wake up because when he pulled the trigger he done himself in, too. You know what I mean? Unless these psychologists they got working on criminals like that, I mean kids in jail because they're too young to go to the gas chamber, unless the psychologist makes him feel not too bad about what he did. I mean, bad enough, bad enough, that's the first step, and then not too bad, so he'll be able to redeem himself."

Athena pushed away the money Naomi was trying to place on the bartender's tray. "When I was sixteen," she said, sipping, "I had it all plotted out to get rid of my dad. He hated everybody even then. There was some people he liked, he wasn't as bad as now but bad enough for me because I felt like I had to grow up to hate people and I didn't want to hate people. I had it all plotted out. Now he's seventy-six, I make custard for him and kiss him and tuck him in at night."

Naomi's eyes began to water from the drink and the embarrassment of hearing a confession.

"Sometimes I think that maybe I should've done it. They would've sent me to Tehachapi Prison for Women. I'd have had a little patch of garden, maybe, and listened to other tales of woe over the sewing machines or the jute mill or whatever they put you to work

on. I would've been out by now, if it was twenty years.
But I mean, there's something about doing something
like that that lifts you out of the rut. While you're
young, I mean." She laughed a long laugh, buoyed up
by the pleasure of being in the bar. "It doesn't mean
anything when you're fifty. No purpose in it. The old
man's not long for this world anyway."

Athena stirred the martini with the toothpick.
"That's why I never had kids. I could have, I was married eleven years, but I figured they'd grow up to hate
me. No, maybe that wasn't the reason, maybe I just
didn't have the courage. Is it courage? What is it?
Maybe I was selfish, but when I look back on those
years, I wonder what I had to be selfish about. You like
kids?"

"My brother Hal, his wife's got a boy, thirteen years
old now. I haven't seen him for a year. Yeah, I like *that*
kid." She sipped. "My brother Cort's going to have
himself some kids. Got married this summer. Met this
girl, love at first sight, got married a month after. He's
the baby of the family. I always think of him as the
baby of the family."

"I feel sorry for kids," Athena mused. "So damn
much to learn. Sometimes you almost snap your cap,
like my own plot."

Naomi found it very hard to lift her gaze to the
tired face across the table. Athena had come to work
in the assessor's office six weeks ago, and this was
the first time they had gone out together after work,
and Naomi was unable to combine in one person the

friendly, joking woman and the woman confessing a plot to murder her father.

Three young men came in, bareheaded, wearing jackets, and hoisted themselves up in a row at the bar, talking loudly, carrying on a humorous argument. One, at the end, leaned around the one in the middle and punched low in the back the one at the other end. The punched one gave a half-laugh, half-moan, jerking his back inward.

"If kids could only see beyond the hump," Athena said. "If they could see that pretty soon they're going to be helping the old man out of the tub. When you're a kid, you couldn't see them with no clothes on and you wouldn't let them see you, your father I mean, and now I help him out of the tub." She laughed through closed lips because she'd put the olive in her mouth.

"Cort married a nice girl," Naomi said, wanting to drop this talk about the terrible things that could have happened when they were young. "Her name's Pauline. She's a typist at the Bon Marché. One time Cort brought her over to meet Mama and she hardly said two words. She wouldn't let Cort hold her hand."

"I got no brother," Athena said. "Got a kid sister, used to have two but one died a couple of years ago, left three kids. The sister I got left lives in Tulsa." She took another sip, began to laugh before she had swallowed it. "I remember one time we were living in Louisville, Kentucky. My dad was working in the tobacco company there, and one night my mom and dad had this awful fight, he said the kid she was pregnant with wasn't his. My sister and me, we held each other in bed. I guess I was about eleven or so. Then he comes in and orders us girls to get up and get our clothes on. Our mom began to beat on his back, and he let her because it wasn't hurting him any, he was a big guy. He piled my sister and me into his Chevy and drove us a hundred miles to some little town where we'd never been and he knocked on a door there. To this day I don't know if he knew those people or not. He won't answer me when I ask, I think he's forgot. He says to the woman who answered the door, he says that 'we hadn't no breakfast and hadn't no money,' and would she give us some breakfast while he looked around for work in that town. She gave us oatmeal, my sister and me. It was the first time I ever ate oatmeal."

"What happened after that?" Naomi asked.

"Oh, after that they got together again and we had another little sister and we all moved out West. Los Angeles."

A warmth came over Naomi, a feeling like love. The woman across the table had become her sister, and nothing was secret between them and nothing was unforgivable. "Our family was real close," she said, carefully because the words wanted to mix themselves up.

"Some families are." Athena looked irritated.

Naomi wondered if what she had said about her own family was taken as a criticism of Athena's family. I ought to be going home, she thought. Mama's alone. What am I doing, sitting here laughing with this woman who almost murdered her father?

"My father was a barber," she heard herself say. "Had a shop where they've got Rich's Cafeteria now. He died of a heart attack when Cort was still almost a baby." Her tongue and lips got in the way of her words. She wanted to say that he was a small man and meticulously neat, she wanted to describe his face and the way he walked and his gentle hands that smelled of cologne, but she couldn't form the words right, and even if she could, respect would prevent her from describing his physical aspects. The memory of him bloomed up here in this place where she ought not to be, and she was a delinquent child whom he had come into the bar for, to fetch home. Hal had gone into bars and Cort went into bars, and that was all right. But what was *she* doing here when she ought to be home with her mother, especially on this day, the day a year ago her brother had died?

"How old's your mother?" Athena asked, and began to laugh again. One of the three young men in a row at the bar turned his head to watch her. "The reason I asked, I had this idea about your mother and my dad. Maybe they could get together."

Naomi watched the young man watching Athena laughing. Athena could not see him. Her friend might be pleased with his interest, Naomi thought, but to her it was not interest in Athena as a woman, it was a contemptuous interest, because the woman was not young, because her sagging throat moved with the laughter, and the gold particles in her teeth shone in the amber light. As she watched the young man watching—a man with a crew cut over his flattish head and wide eyes in a small face—a desire rose up in her to protect her friend with love, to protect even the young punk, to protect everybody with a love that would submerge all contempt. He saw her watching him and turned his gaze on her, and a many-fingered lightning raced across her belly.

"We ought to arrange it so they'd get married," Athena was saying. "One time I tried to get him to go into a rest home. I told him he'd have lots of friends, but he wouldn't budge. So I thought, what the hell, let him have his own way, take care of him, give me something to do in the evening besides file my fingernails."

A seeking look in Athena's large eyes shocked Naomi, and she fumbled around in her conscience for the right response. In her friend's eyes was a desperate need to be instructed in the rigors of her own old age coming, a need to be solaced even by the picayune face of Naomi, by Naomi, who was ignorant of what everybody else knew. But Naomi could console only her own, only Mama and Cort. She heard herself laughing, she bent her head down to the rickety table, laughing at the joke that Athena had already left far behind. "Oh, they'd make a couple all right!" she agreed.

"You girls think of something funny?" the young punk asked.

"We just arranged a marriage," Athena said.

"For you?"

"Oh, yes, for me!" Athena, laughing, almost choked on the smoke of her cigarette.

"Well, why not?" he asked, his eyes closing for an instant to hide the taunting in them, his mouth smiling acceptingly. "Why not?"

Athena was pounding her chest to bring up the smoke. "Don't ask me why not so many times or I'll tell you why not!"

Naomi, impressed by her friend's rejection of the young punk's ridicule, bowed her head to the table again, laughing, taken over by pleasure with her own life. She was who she had chosen to be, a county courthouse clerk, unmarried, going home in a minute to her mother.

The sky was dark when she got off the bus and walked the three blocks to home. "Mama," she called, unlocking the door, accidentally kicking a small sample box of cereal left on the porch. With the door open, her hand on the knob, she stooped to pick up the box. On it was the face of a happy squirrel wearing a bow tie. "Mama," she called, "somebody left something for you."

Her mother was lying on the sofa, covered by the afghan, her face pale in the flicker and waves of blue light from the television screen. No light was on anywhere in the rest of the house. "Where you been?"

"I did some shopping."

"Today's the day he died." Her mother lifted her

arms, and Naomi sank down and gathered up the old body grown so thin in the past year. But her mother thrust her away. The smell of the bar was on her.

Naomi pushed herself up and stood unsteadily, took off her hat, took off her coat, stepped out of her high-heeled shoes. She had been reminded for over a month that this Friday was the date he had died a year ago. She had known it herself without reminders. Without any warning in herself, a wail came up, and more wails, sounding like wails of remorse to appease her mother. Unable to do anything about them, she could only wonder. They weren't over her brother, nor over her mother, and she didn't know what they were over, unless they were over herself.

5

Dolores left the city a few days after high-school grad-uation exercises, boarding the bus to San Francisco. She found a place to live in an apartment shared by three other girls. It was a first-floor apartment, old, heavily carpeted, the living room full of potted plants, the mantelpiece laden with dime-store china figures. They took turns cleaning the kitchen and vacuuming the living room that nobody used. Above them lived more girls, and on the third floor, the top, lived the landlady, a Frenchwoman who came down to investi-gate complaints and to make complaints of her own. Her rooms for girls were known to agencies for im-migrants, to the French consul, and were advertised in the "For Rent" columns, and no more than a day passed between the vacating of a room and the renting of it. At the time Dolores moved into the front bed-room that faced the street, two French girls were living in the bedrooms down the hall, one a secretary at the consulate and the other a typist for an importer, and the fourth bedroom was rented to a girl from Chicago, a cocktail waitress, who made use of the extra closet in the living room to hang up the clothes her own closet couldn't hold and to set out shoes in a row, shoes with heels fantastically high—lucite heels and gilt heels and electric-blue suede heels and red lacquered heels.

"Oh, you are so *attracteef!*" Janine, the consular secretary, told Dolores the first day. Chatting over coffee in the small kitchen, Dolores began to sense sharply the appraising that women do of one another. Janine was observing Dolores's womanness, everything about her—her skin, her features, her hands, her legs, her hair, particulars even more meaningful than they had been to the men in her mother's cafe back home, and Dolores felt the presence of the thousands of women in the city, the women by whom she would be measured and against whom she would measure herself. The eyes of this woman showed a degree more of keenness than that in men's eyes, a desperation, a touch of despair, and Dolores felt trapped by this woman across the table, this flattering woman constantly pushing up the sleeves of her soiled pongee kimono, tossing back her short dark hair.

Dolores found a job as waitress in a small restaurant serving expensive lunches on white tablecloths, and in her third week there accepted an invitation to take a ride around the city from a gray-haired, bustling man, a contractor who joked with her almost every day, snuffling his laughter down his nose. Back home, small-time contractors came into her mother's cafe in clothes the color of concrete dust and complained about unions, lumberyards, architects, owners, and banks. This one wore tailored suits and parked his red and white Corvette at the foot of a hill and pointed out to her an apartment building at the top, its windows hot gold in the setting sun, or parked before a modern house, square, a great reflective expanse of glass facing the bay, or before a stark, concrete church, a neon cross dividing its triangular front. Once, when they were parked on a hill that gave a view of the Embarcadero, she expected him to say that the white ship alongside a pier was his, like an exuberant child would say to an adult in tow. But she saw that *she* was the child, believing that a city grew up by itself, magically. Not only did he alter the skyline, change the views of the city, he knew about scandals in city politics, and those involved in the scandals were friends or enemies of his; he patronized the best restaurants and the jazz clubs, and pointed out to her which innocuous houses had once been famous houses of prostitution.

Her first time out with him he had explained that his wife was away for a couple of weeks and he needed to hear a woman laughing and to help her put on her coat, and she laughed at the comedy they saw and gracefully moved her shoulders for the coat. The evening was his way of telling her he missed his wife. The following night he parked his car in the Marina, and while the masts of the sailboats swayed across the windshield, he spent two hours caressing her. She prepared for the third evening by dropping scented balls of oil, like somber-colored jewels, into her bath water, by changing earrings three times and lipstick twice, by drawing mascara lines around her eyes, fascinated by the effect of each artifice.

"You are stunning!" Janine clapped her hands, muttering something in French, like a prayer. "Who is he? Who is the man? Is he a movie star?"

Dolores sat at the kitchen table and, over a cup of black coffee, told Janine about him while the woman muttered prayers in French and allowed her pongee kimono to fall open at her breasts.

"Oh, he is a man of distinction," Janine said. "That is the kind of man you deserve. You have an *expenseef* look," laughing with an excess of pleasure that proved the laughter false.

The flattery was demanding something of Dolores. She couldn't reject it because she needed even flattery's imitation of praise. It demanded that she confirm the truth of it and surprise this woman with the truth. Toying with her teaspoon, her voice low, she said, "There was a man back home, he was an attorney, he was running for Congress. I mean he was very intelligent and everybody liked him, and he killed himself over me. I mean he was in love with me. He had a wife and child."

Janine lifted her dark eyes to stare, and a tangle of noises came into her throat, a seductive laugh entangled with a moan. "Ah, no, that is *terrible*! Poor man! Poor man! I could tell when I saw you. Whenever you see a beautiful girl who is sad, you can say to yourself, 'Some man has wounded her, he is tied to his wife's apron strings and he did not have the courage to untie himself.' That is the way it is. But with you I saw something more, something tragic. I said to myself, 'There was violence. The man shot his wife.' And then it came to me, 'No, he shot himself. That girl has that look of losing what she can *nevair* get back.'"

"You knew about me?"

"I looked and I knew."

"You mean I didn't even have to tell you?"

"That is *why* you told me. Because I knew already. You could see in my face that I knew. All my life I have this intuition. It has *nevair* disappointed me. *Nevair.* Have you also felt intuition? *They* do not have it, men do not have it. Only women. It is mysterious, who knows where it comes from? That is why they look up to us. When a man takes a woman out, as tonight this man will take you out, he will be in awe of you. Because you have the intuition. They envy us for it. We have this gift while *they*," and she clapped a hand to her head, "they *think* and they *think* how to figure out somebody, who to trust and who not to trust, but the woman, *she* has the answer just like that," snapping her fingers. "You have intuition about this man?"

"George, you mean?"

"That is his name? You have intuition there will be trouble?"

"He's married, if that's what you mean."

"Married or not! Sometime there is no trouble at

all with the married ones. I am talking about how you *feel . . .*"

"You mean am I in love with him?"

"No, no, no! I am asking—do you feel trouble is coming?"

"Not exactly."

"Well, good then. That is good. You have a nice time and do not worry." Janine's eyes were luminous— she had revealed herself. She was a seeress, she knew about Dolores's past and future, and her thin mouth smiled a false apology for her intrusion into another person's life.

Dolores's heels, clicking sharply on the sidewalk from the Corvette to the door of his apartment building, were silenced by the thick carpet of the foyer. Silence now, like the unspeaking moment before the embrace. They hurried in silence up the stairs and past the doors of other tenants, doors he must have entered with his wife for an evening's visit, and came at last to his door.

A lamp was on in the small entry. He went before her into the living room, switching on another lamp. "Come on, come in, don't stand there like a country cousin," he called back to her. He did not help her take off her coat, as he had done in restaurants and theaters, and she dropped it on the long beige couch. "Want some coffee?" he asked, drawing curtains together across the expanse of glass, closing out the reflection of the large white lamp he had lit. The moment's reflection of the lamp had intrigued her—the lamp it-self was his, but the reflection of it, like a lamp out in the night, was hers. "Come on, let's have some coffee. Something else, see what we can find. Usually some fish eggs around, put 'em on crackers."

Her heels still silenced by carpet, this one the color of sand and that sent up a thick, stuffy feeling into her legs, she followed him toward the kitchen. At the kitchen doorway he turned, impetuously, fitfully, to watch her cross the room, a nervous, embarrassed smile in his eyes. "Come on," he said, taking in how she looked in his apartment, a girl whose face was excitingly unfa-miliar and whose body he was to know in a little while.

She followed him into the small, gleaming kitchen, and sat down at the glass-top table. Through the glass she saw her legs and how her short black dress slipped up past her knees as she crossed them. He tossed his cigarettes onto the table. Every time, before, he had brought out the pack gracefully, a wordless, confiden-tial, insinuating offer. She did not touch them. She put her elbows on the table and her chin in her hands and watched him opening jars, stooping to look for crack-ers in a low cupboard, measuring coffee for the tall chromium percolator.

"That thing looks like a rocket," she said, and he laughed, a quick, eager laugh to make them both feel at home.

"It does, it does," he agreed, talking so fast as he counted spoonfuls that his teeth caught at the words. He's fifty, she thought, and he talks as fast as a kid.

Some coffee grounds scattered over the top of the stove, and he glanced at her sideways to see if she had noticed.

"You nervous?" she asked, laughing.

"Naw, naw, I hate this teaspoon stuff. I hate little bitsy stuff. I'm a mountain mover, like to move big things fast. You know what I've always had in mind to do? Move New York to San Francisco and vice versa. Lots of people I know in New York are never going to get out here, so I could do that little favor for them. No more blizzards in winter, no more steam baths in summer."

"I like this city where it is," she said, implying that she was already rooted there, making the entire strange, confusing city her own so that she might feel less homeless now in his apartment, less vulnerable to him.

"What's the matter with you, you don't like to move around?" He was glancing at her derisively. "You come up from Fresno? San Bernardino? and that's the big move in your life? Got no ambition?" He set out a jar of caviar, crackers on a plate, little silver knives, and jerked out the other chair. "Go ahead, eat," he said, biting a cracker in two. The black caviar slid down his tongue. "I like women with ambition. The only trouble with my wife, it made her kind of shrill, you know what I mean? When I first met her it was fine, she was restless, she had to be the best in everything and that meant bed, too, and that was fine. But after a while the ambition destroyed the woman in her. What you've got to remember is not to let it destroy you but you've got to have it in you. You just want to be a waitress all your life?"

She had no answer. Why should she drag up

wishes enmeshed in her life, unformed wishes that were a part of her being, and give them as answers to his nervous hounding of her? She sensed that he was talking so fast and so compulsively, jamming crackers and caviar into his mouth, because he felt on the spot and wanted her there instead.

"Is that it?" he persisted.

"I don't know what I want," she said.

"You want to marry a fry cook and get yourself six kids?"

"Maybe," she said. The caviar was too fishy and black. She had never eaten the stuff before and could not make herself like it while beset by his heckling in this kitchen that belonged to his wife.

"Don't you like it?"

"Not much."

"You marry a fry cook and eat french fries and fried eggs every meal. You like that better?"

"No."

The suspense, the desire for him was fading from her face, from her gestures. She saw his face go blank with confusion. He laid his fingertips over hers, attempting a delicate approach. "Come on, smile," he said. "Ah, that's great, the sun is shining again. My wife's in Palm Springs," supping up his coffee. "She went down to L.A. to push accounts down there and took a little vacation afterwards. I think she got somebody with her, some guy from San Diego. How I can tell, I phoned her tonight and she sounded happy. When she's alone anywhere she sounds like a kid. Cries."

"She must be awfully smart to run a business. My mother has this cafe, but that's nothing compared to what your wife does. How many people work for your wife?"

"She runs that business like a man. I set her up with the capital, and in seven years she's made it into a big thing. Galatea, Inc. That's a lousy name, I said. What about Linda Lou? What about Dolores Dee? That's what I said—what about Dolores? But she wanted that Galatea. So the best shops in the country carry Galatea lingerie. She was my secretary but she turned out to be so smart I had to marry her. I guess she's got about fifty people in the factory." He took off his glasses to wipe them with the yellow linen napkin, holding them down on his stomach, farsightedly. "See? She's got a business, she's got a name, but she's unhappy because she figures she's not woman enough. She'd take one look at you, she'd be envious."

He wanted her to believe that he *knew* women, she saw that. He wanted her to believe he knew *her,* the girl across the table, and that if there was anything she didn't know about herself she had only to ask him and he'd tell her. He was wiping his glasses on and on, gazing at her with exposed eyes, the exposed face without glasses bringing instantly nearer the time of exploring and exposure.

"She was miserable in Mexico," he said. "The women there are so voluptuous, Jesus. She's built like a sparrow. She had to do something to attract attention so she went into a beauty shop and had her hair colored pink. Pink. That got her the stares. Someday how'd you like to go down there with me? There's a motel in Hermosillo, got a swimming pool like a harem pool, beautiful tile, outdoors, pillars in the water, and all lit up at night. You swim in there at midnight, warm, feel like you're living. They got a deer that wanders around on the grass, eats out of your hand." He slipped on his glasses, got up. The time was near. "Come on, you want to hear some music? You like jazz? Stravinsky?"

She got up, holding her small gold leather purse under her breasts, and followed him, puzzled now by his nervous delaying.

"Got a Giuffre record here," he said, twirling knobs on a long, low, blond wood cabinet, setting down record and needle, all with his back to her. "You like him? You ever heard him?" The music began to ricochet around the room. "Sit down," he said. "Listen to this guy on the bass. Listen." Over his shoulder he was watching her. "What's the matter, you think you're a cat or something, got to think about every chair? Sit on the couch. Listen, they're good, uh?" Leaning back against the cabinet, he watched her sit down. "They're good, uh?" he said, coming to her, at last, sitting down by her, laying his hand on the black silk over her stomach, running his lips around the rim of her ear. "Come on, come on, it's bedtime."

Awkwardly, because he was holding her against him, she entered the bedroom, a room of pale colors and rich and various textures, a room that, though it was shared by him, was a woman's room. Lustrous chalk-white curtains hung in pure stillness from ceiling to curly beige carpet. The headboard of the bed was a great whorl of gilded plaster with a gilded cherub's head in the center, and gold threads gleamed here and there in the heavy white silk spread. She was afraid of the woman's wrath. She was afraid and felt sympathy, yet found pleasure in her own desirability, herself so coveted that he had brought her here to the bed he shared with his wife. She stepped out of her shoes and came down to his height. At the same moment he embraced her, she felt a trembling begin at the core of him.

"Sit here, sit here," he said, and sat her down on the bench before the oval mirror in an ornate frame, and, standing behind her, he fumbled the hairclasp out and, when her hair was down, slipped her dress off her shoulders. She could not glance at herself in the mirror because the mirror was not hers and had held the image of his wife, but she could glance up at his reflection as he went about undressing her, his gray head bowed toward the mirror, and in that moment her dislike of him overcame her. Who was he but a blundering, trembling, fast-talking fifty-year-old man whose gray hair was bouncing lifelessly as he bent forward toward the mirror to lift in his hand the breast he had uncovered and watch how it moved in his moving fingers. But her dislike of him frightened her, she saw him as she did not want to see him. The signs of his weakness laid her down again beside Hal Costigan, now knowing beforehand that he was to take his life. She wanted to see this man as he had been before this night, when his gray hair had a life to it, and the body in its fine suit a strength to it, and his face a cleverness and an assurance of all he had accomplished. With sudden urgency she turned to him and took his face in her hands and kissed him. She heard a moan come into his mouth and stay baffled there because it had no escape.

When his wife returned, three days later, he came to Dolores's room for the first time. All was quiet at midnight, the other girls asleep. She switched on the light in her room before she dropped the Venetian blinds, and anyone glancing out a window across the street or up from the sidewalk could have seen him there in her room, and that possibility annoyed him. The girls had men of their own sometimes: the cocktail waitress had opened her door for a departing lover at five in the morning at the same moment Dolores had opened hers to go to the bathroom, and Janine on Saturday nights had her slight, sad-faced American lover. But the stories she had told him of the other girls and their lovers must have contributed to his discomfort. He said the place had a "transient atmosphere." He made love to her quickly, smoked half a cigarette, and left. She did not see him for a week, and then one day as she was climbing the stairs after work she heard the phone ringing on the table in the hallway.

Within an hour he came by, and drove for another hour to Sonoma, over the bridge and north. They ate supper in a flashy restaurant that she knew was not the best in the town, and two blocks away they found a motel. Its green neon sign blinked on and off around the edges of the blind in the small dark room. He was more curious, more experimental than he had been in his own bed, and she felt that he was living a lascivious dream, materialized for him by the cheap motel and the girl who complied with his dream. But on the long ride home through the stretch of darkness, he seemed not to remember or to be grateful for his dream come true. He talked about city politics, labor racketeers. She was afraid that they meant nothing to each other, after all. His talk, now, about events in which she did not figure, told her clearly that he did not require her in his life. The night she had gone up to his apartment, she had felt that she was entering some opulent state—his mistress, more beloved than his wife, set up in an apartment of her own and adorned by couturier dresses, by real jewels. The fact that the motel was not high class, that the room smelled of disinfectant, that silverfish raced over the bathroom tile, and that he talked to her now of things that cut all threads with the intimacy in the motel—these facts, she told herself, had no bearing on their future. She lifted his right hand from the steering wheel and kissed the back of it and between the fingers.

But three more weeks went by, and he did not suggest that she look for an apartment of her own, and he brought no gifts. Instead, he drove her habitually to a motel on the beach, south of the city. Up a short dirt road off the highway, a small white frame motel and a row of cabins stood isolated by the rocky cliffs and the sea and sky. They returned each time to the same cabin and plugged in the electric heater for warmth. The orange glow of the wires in the battered cylindrical heater filled the room with a dim, coppery light, and the sound of the sea struck a great echo, far out. Across the highway, a seed company's acres of flowers were blooming, and their fragrance was blown in through the cracks, permeating the cabin when the wind was still, and in those times of being with him there, she longed to be in love with him. Her resentment of him for bringing no gifts had to be banked down because if he suspected that she wanted more of him than himself making love to her, he might drop her. The loving was enough. All she needed she had in these nights in the sand-shifted shack.

Some nights the music from the jukebox in the motel bar blew down past the row of cabins. A man's voice singing took her by surprise, and she lay afraid of intrusion, convinced the singer himself was coming down the path. Or the muted notes of a saxophone, heard above the subsiding sound of the waves, was the voice of a lover in another cabin, amplified by a mystical trick. The music was a reminder to her of the closeness of others at the bar who knew by the red car parked behind the cabin that a couple was inside. When a man and woman came along the row one night, the woman muffling a high laugh, it seemed to Dolores, lying on the rented bed in the dim, wire-lit room, that at last the curious were stealing down the path to peer in under the curtains.

"What you scared of?" he asked in her ear. "You close up like a little ol' morning glory when it isn't time yet."

But the couple on the path had intruded, bringing with them her complaints against him. If she asked for gifts, it was only because she wanted them as evidence that she was more than a pretty waitress taken out to a shack on the beach. But if she asked, he might turn cold and cruel instantly, take his face from her face, his body from her body, and leave her alone and ashamed of her need for anything more than the few hours, the few nights with him.

"Come on, what you scared of? They don't rent the same cabin to two couples. They went in already."

She closed her eyes against his impatient eyes that could not take a moment to wonder. She lifted her mouth to his as a way of asking him to stay with her, and she asked his forgiveness for her complaints by drawing from his mouth all his anger, every cruel word that he might say, and by being as he wanted her to be for the rest of the time; and when they lay apart, what she was asking for changed back again. If she brought him pleasure, wasn't it natural that he tell her so with gifts? It must be natural, so many women were given gifts by the men who loved them for the pleasure they gave. If she never complained, then she was cheap. She was nothing but a dumb waitress who went to bed with him for nothing.

"I guess you think I'm a fool," she said.

"A fool?" He was already sitting with his back to her, rubbing the sole of his foot before he pulled on his sock.

"Because I come here for nothing."

"What do you mean for nothing?" so swiftly she suspected his answer had been ready for weeks. "Don't you like it? You act like you like it."

How would other women say, *that's not enough*? With what words, in what way? "That's not enough," she said.

"I'm not man enough for you? What you want, some nature boy? Jack Biceps?"

"That's not what I mean." Was he trying to cuff her away from her real meaning by pretending to be hurt by what she didn't mean? "What I mean is, you never bring me anything." But, spoken at last, it wasn't what she meant, either.

"Like what? Like what?"

Her fear of being discarded by this man who was more to her now than any man had ever been, even more than Hal, took away her wishes, leaving her only a trace of a complaint. "Like little things."

"What little things?"

"Like big things."

"What then? Big things or little things? Make up your mind." Though he continued with his dressing, his clothes appeared not to be his own. With distaste he examined his shirt as if suspecting someone of borrowing it and returning it unclean.

"It depends on how much you like me. If you like me a lot, they're little things." She was shameless, forcing him to weigh and measure her value to him.

"Give me an example."

"Like a place, like an apartment . . ."

"Anything else?"

"You shouldn't ask me to list them."

"Why not? Don't you like to list them?"

"No." She had made a mistake. She didn't need anything more from him, not anything more than her numb, kneaded mouth whose lipstick was gone, its color, chosen with care for its promise of love, now a barely present coloring over the rest of her face, not anything more than the clamoring of her body for him, waking her up in the night, back in her own room.

"Go on."

"No."

"You sorry you started it?"

She stuffed some ends of her hair into her mouth and began to cry, confused by her contradictory wishes.

"What's the crying for?" patting her stomach.

She twisted a strand of hair around her fingers, close to her face. "There was a man who killed himself over me," she wept. "You think I'm nobody, but there was a man who fell in love with me."

"No, hell, I don't think you're nobody," patting. "What do you mean, he killed himself?"

"Just what I said."

"All right, all right. But I'm a little deaf. I don't get it."

"You want me to say it again?"

"If it doesn't hurt too much."

"I said he killed himself."

"How did that happen?"

"It happened, it happened."

"Sure it did, sure it did. Just tell me how."

"He was married, and he had a little boy," covering her mouth with her hair.

"Yuh, go on," patting.

"He knew we were going to be found out but he didn't care."

"Yuh?"

"He didn't care."

"Listen, sweetie, listen, doll," he said. "You must have left something out."

"What?"

"You tell *me* what. I don't want to hurt your tender feelings, but it doesn't seem like that's enough reason for a man to kill himself over."

"You don't know the whole story!"

"That's exactly what I'm saying."

"He was running for Congress," she explained, with as much insulting, indignant enunciation as she could scare up for her small, broken voice, "and we were found out a few days before election day. What I'm saying is he didn't care about the election, I mean if he had to kill himself. What I'm saying is that he couldn't help it if he was in love with me."

"Sounds funny to me," he said. "Oh, you're telling the truth, you're telling the truth as you see it. But a man doesn't do that, I mean go out of his mind for wanting some girl unless he's out of his mind already." He turned his back on her again to tie his shoes. When he straightened up he consulted his wristwatch. "Quarter to twelve," he said. "Time to get up."

She placed a palm over her nipple to hide a spangle of pain that she imagined was detectable by him. He was taking away from her all that she had tried to claim for herself in her story about Hal Costigan, the image of herself as a girl desirable beyond any risk. With his mockery, he was taking that story away just as she was telling it for the first time to any man, and here, under her palm, her nipple's small begging voice was calling him back.

Standing above her, he dropped her underwear and slip over her crossed hands. "Come on, come on. What're you looking like a madonna for? Are you Catholic? You sore at me because I said your story doesn't make sense?" He dropped her dress over her stomach, covering up everything he had wanted uncovered before. Her nylons he dropped on her thighs.

"You're not so great," she heard herself say, low.

"Hell, I know I'm not so great," pretending good humor about his deficiencies.

"You could die, too," she said.

"I know all about it," shrugging on his coat.

"You could shoot yourself."

"Yeah, I could if I got cancer or something."

"You could do it anyway."

"Who knows?" he said, agreeably.

With angry flicks of her hand, she tossed aside the clothes, sat up, and began to dress. "You're not so great."

"Nobody ever told you I was, did they?" He went to the window, drew back the curtain, and, with a hand at each temple, peered out through the glass. "I can see the waves," he said. "The foam, the white part on the breakers. You ever see that old movie where the guy walks out into the ocean? Can't swim, just keeps on walking out into the ocean? Maybe that's the way I'd do it if I was going to do it. If I get to thinking about how not so great I am, like you want me to." He chuckled. "Unless I get worried about sharks."

She glanced up as she dressed and saw her reflection in the window he was peering through, the reflection of the half-clad girl imposing itself between him and the darkness. With her dress held to her breasts she gazed at his back, at his gray head bent forward so his brow touched the glass, and at her almost transparent self in the pane, and shame came over her for asking something of this man who was as vulnerable as Hal Costigan to dying. The girl in the glass stood between him and the night, just as she had between Hal and the night.

He turned and stood waiting, hands in his pockets jingling coins and keys, and she knew when she glanced at his face and saw him gazing at nothing that the bitter taste in her mouth was in his, the same.

6

Toward midnight Cort's wife felt the labor pains come faster. She was walking through the house, and every time the pains came she knelt down. She knelt down by the bed where Cort was lying, and when the pain passed she looked up at him, and he saw the frown, the knot of pain, ease from her face. The contractions had kept her awake the night before and most of the day, and her face was very pale, and he saw in her eyes only a remote need of him. Her fear of the ordeal that was near left him out.

Wrapped in her coat, she leaned against him in the car, and when the cramps came he stroked her thigh. Most of the houses were dark. He had always been disturbed by the presence of so many people asleep, by the blocks and blocks of flimsy houses into which the darkness flowed. Everyone seemed at the mercy of so many things, and again the memory of his brother came to him as it had come so often in the past few weeks. The memory of his brother came to him vividly now as he drove his wife through the streets of the sleeping city. For a moment, a hallucination that his brother was sitting on the other side of his wife caused him to slip his arm around her shoulders and kiss her hair.

She was given a bed in the labor room, in a row of four beds. Down the row, a young woman with pink curlers in her hair was chatting with her husband, who was sitting in a chair by her bed. But Cort's wife, who hadn't slept for almost twenty-four hours, was given a sedative by a tired young doctor. She spoke just a few words to Cort and began to drowse.

Cort went out, under a stucco portico, past a trickling fountain, and around plots of flowers. He walked past the emergency entrance, under its red light, past the wing of the building and its rows of lighted windows. It was the last few hours of their being two, he and his wife, the last hours of a closeness he suspected would never return when the child entered the picture, and he resented the stranger child who was to intrude on the intimacy of the parents and claim some of the love, or even all, from the tall, long-legged woman with her sullen, bony face that could focus on a kiss and draw out of him the brooding left by his brother. He loved her for her healing of him, he loved the woman asleep in that high bed on which other women in labor had lain, and he needed her more than would the stranger of a child. A desperate desire came over him to return with her to the beginning, to take her home with her belly flat and no child anywhere, a desire for her unhindered, undivided, fresh and startling, healing of him as she had been at the beginning, because, contending with her now and with the child, was his brother, following him step for step in the night.

Under an elm tree lit by a lamp hanging high above the street, he waited for his brother to take the last step to him, and, when the presence of the dead man was full upon him, he struck the trunk of the tree to punish himself with pain because he, Cort, was a criminal and nobody knew it. It was a crime to bring a child into the world and not love life yourself. It was a crime to hold out to the child a hand that had no meaning to offer, and to lead the child into life. He stood on the curb, crying noiselessly with fatigue and anxiety and the desire to return his wife alone and without child to the past.

Leaf shadows, enlarged to enormous size by the high globe, lay all around him, intensifying his feeling of unreality, and he sat down on the curb in their midst and lit a cigarette to smoke out the tears from his throat. How often in the past year he had called up his brother! Even in the midst of pleasure, he had brought him into the company and introduced him around to remind them all of the meaninglessness of their existence. Six weeks ago on a Sunday afternoon, Pauline and he were guests at a neighbor's outdoor party; the odor of barbecued meat floated over the yard, smoke swirled out from the brick barbecue, and the fragrance of liquor rose up from the cold glass in his hand. He was sitting by a lattice that cast a striped

shadow over him—he liked that puzzling shadow—
and his wife was reclining close by on a canvas chair.
By him were three men, all with glasses in their hands.
He knew none of them, they were friends of the host,
but given a lead by a word, by a pause, he had told
them about his brother, he had lauded his brother to
the smoky sky. No one so sensitive, no one so intelligent, no one with the courage to say what he'd said
in his act of suicide, oh, the greatest guy in the world!
They had nodded or gazed at him, but one man had
wandered away, and later, when the party was breaking up, Cort had caught sight of him. Their eyes met,
and the antagonism in the man's eyes had shocked
him. On the curb now, in the midst of the giant leaf
shadows, he remembered the times when he and his
wife had gone to movies with other couples and as
they all sat crowded together in a booth in a bar, he
had recalled his brother. He told about his brother
every chance he got, like a derelict who claims high-
class relatives. He had to tell everybody that he, Cort,
was different, he was smarter than his listeners, who
accepted life without questioning. With knuckles that
were still crumpled with pain, he struck the elm tree
again, then spread his stinging, jerking fingers over
his knee, waiting until they calmed.

He got up, crossed to the other corner, and walked
along by the old two-story frame houses that made
up this neighborhood where wealthy, elderly women
lived, where lawns were hedged in and lace curtains
hung in windows that looked out onto high porches

and wicker chairs. An exotic tree of waxy white blooms confronted him at the edge of a yard, overbearing in its still, heavy beauty. From somewhere came the fragrance of orange blossoms and from somewhere the fragrance of wisteria, and it seemed to him that fragrances in this neighborhood of the elderly were like children who had wandered over from another part of the city where children slept two and three and four in a bedroom and no bedroom was unused, as bedrooms were unused in these tall houses. Maybe, he thought, the child, the wandering fragrance, would assist the mother in the task of eradicating the image of the dead brother from the heart of the father. Maybe the child would be an ally. But what a job he was assigning the child at the moment of its birth. The child was to give the father a reason for living! It would never be equal to the task. The task was the father's, the task of the father was to give himself and the child a reason. Not love yet, but the possibility of love caused him now to protect the child from the harm the father might do it. He heard in his throat his plea to his brother to go, to stop hounding him, to disappear on this spot, and leave him, younger brother, alone.

Unwilling to go back to the maternity ward and wait there, he walked on, wanting to go instead to his sister, Naomi, wanting to knock on the kitchen door and ask for a cup of coffee. He wanted to know, for the first time, if she felt the same way about Hal that he felt. He had never even wondered before if that which had been done to him had also been done to her. Only

Naomi—he wanted to see his sister alone, he wanted his mother to be asleep, so he and his sister could talk very quietly in the kitchen. But what could *she* do for him? Naomi, simple, awkward, skittish woman? What could he say to her when he was convinced beforehand that she would not comprehend? She had idolized their brother, their brother could do no wrong, not even in that final act.

Crying in his throat for a love of life to exorcise the dead man, he wandered out into the street. A dog up on a porch growled at him, growled a late-night threat, safe under a hammock or a chair.

7

They sat down, tugged off their gloves, took off their hats.

"You girls are getting to be regulars." The bartender clucked his tongue. "Every damn week."

Naomi sat with her back to the entrance. At the table behind Athena a man sat alone, his glass down on an open newspaper. He had lifted his head, slowly alerted, amused by their entrance.

"What do your husbands say when you come home late, no supper, nothing?" the bartender asked.

"That's why we got no husbands. They gripe too much." With elbows resting on the table, Athena ran her fingers through the curls above her ears, bowing her head quickly to do it. "Isn't that right, Naomi?" winking at her.

"Naomi what?" the man at the table asked, gazing at her past Athena, who turned around to see him.

"Costigan," said Athena.

"You from Butte, Montana?" the man asked Naomi.

"I had a sister by that name. She left home at sixteen and we never heard a word from her."

"I'm from right here," Naomi said.

"Native daughter," Athena said.

"It ain't often you hear the name Naomi," he said.

"It isn't often you hear my name, either," said Athena. "I think my old man named me after some Greek goddess."

"I got a name everybody else's got," he said. "Or it sounds like that. I'll tell you if you don't laugh."

"We won't laugh." Athena was acting strange, her voice had a crackling sound, and her body seemed rich with pleasure.

"Dan O'Leary," he said. "Do I look like one?"

"Like what?" Athena asked.

"Like a Dan O'Leary."

"If you gave me any other name I'd think you were kidding me," she said.

"You know what his real name is?" the bartender said. "Adolf Hitler. He never really died."

"Yeah, I'm looking for work over here," said Dan O'Leary, and he laughed half a dozen staccato sounds. "Dirty work."

"What kind of work do you do?" Athena asked.

"Well," he said, "I've been a pants presser, ship's steward, I've been a funny man in a burlesque show, and I also barked. You know, stand out in front and bark," and he barked like a dog.

Athena's laugh was loud and crackly.

"That was the most low-down job of all, barking

like that," he said. "But a princess rescued me. Princess Nadja. She was the stripper and she fell in love with me. She set me up in business for myself, opened a little bar for me."

"You go broke?" asked Athena.

"Me go broke?" He seemed offended. "It wasn't me that went broke. The bar went broke."

"What happened to Princess Nadja? She get mad at you?" Athena turned her chair so that she could talk to both Naomi and the man, and crossed her legs.

"Nobody gets mad at me," he said. "It ain't in my nature for people to get mad at me. No, she didn't get mad. I just left her. She was loony about white and it gave me the creeps."

"What's white?" asked Athena, puzzled.

"Every goddamn thing white. She got some crazy fixation on white. Is that what you call it?" he asked Naomi, implying that since she spoke less she knew more. "It begun to bug me. Every damn rug in the house was white, every damn lamp, every damn everything, and her hair is also pearly white. It's real nice for a while, feel like you're living on the moon. But after a while it begun to bug me. I said to her, you ain't fooling me, baby, you sit on the toilet like everybody else—excuse me, girls. I said, you trying to look pure or something, and I spilled a gallon of dago wine in the middle of the living room rug. I don't do things like that habitually, you understand." He leaned forward on his elbows, speaking to Naomi. "You follow me or you think I'm bats?"

Athena turned back to their own table, laughing. "You're bats!"

He smiled at Naomi, a pale, lopsided smile, his eyes aware of his mouth's pleading. "That don't hurt me," he said. "As long as I'm bats and funny. If I was bats and sad, you'd have every right to turn me in."

Naomi disliked his singling her out to talk to, a homely woman who had to be treated with respect, who had to be talked to for a few moments to relieve his tension from talking to Athena, the woman he wanted to talk to. But she wondered—was he saying to her, past Athena, that between himself and herself was an unspoken understanding requiring no jokes? You're a crazy woman, she said to herself. He got to sleep with a woman other men pay to see undress herself. You're not a woman to him and Athena's not a woman, and he gets a kick out of making us believe he thinks we're real attractive women. He gets a kick out of hearing a couple of gullible women laugh their cackling, girlish laughs. She pulled on her gloves.

"Hey, you're not going?" he said.

Usually she had a smart remark to make to the men who came into the recorder's office and teased her with their insinuations that she was somebody and that if they had the courage, the recklessness, they'd leave their wives for her. She didn't want to answer that way to this man, but she did. "I'm afraid of the dark," she said.

"Of the dark?" He wagged his head. "God Almighty, she says she's afraid of the dark." His face lapsed into petulant resentment, and she realized that even the dumbest woman, leaving him in the midst of his act, could hurt his feelings. "God Almighty," he said, "something's wrong. Here this woman comes into a bar and she got to leave before it gets dark. Everybody think they're two years old?"

When they left, she saw that he was still wagging his head. It was the first time ever she had hurt a man. She had hurt him inadvertently, but all evening, at home, she was troubled by contending feelings, by a sense of her own power and by a sense of guilt, and, lying in bed, a crazy fear that she had ruined her chances with him took hold of her.

She saw him again the next day. He was at the other side of the horseshoe-shaped lunch counter in the drugstore, and when she looked up from the menu and saw him across the space where the waitress flitted around, he began to shake his head again, unbelievingly, chidingly. He was again the man whom nobody could get mad at because he got mad at nobody. He carried his coffee and sandwich carefully around the counter and sat down by her, and he learned, that noon, who she was because she sat there with her hands trembling on her cup.

A few minutes before it was time to put on her coat, he came into the recorder's office. With his hands in his pockets, he glanced along the shelves of red and gray record books, his manner that of one who finds no place too exclusive for him to enter. She slipped her coat on, buttoning it up to her chin, and he opened the door for her and walked along beside her down the hall, limping.

"You never knew I had a bullet in my knee, did you?" he asked. He had not limped when they walked out of the drugstore together, and she knew he was pretending to limp now.

"I got this hotel room almost in the center of town, so I don't need to ride any buses to get to where the action is. So I figured it'd be interesting just to ride a bus, but I didn't want any old line, like the B or the G. It's got to be your bus with you on it. Then you can point out what you think I ought to see, like the high school, you know? What's the population of this town, would you say?" They stood on the edge of the crowd waiting for the buses across from the courthouse.

"Maybe a hundred thousand," she said.

"They all catch the bus at this hour?"

She laughed, and he bent over to grip his knee. "Don't make me laugh," he said. "My knee buckles."

He limped behind her aboard the bus and half fell into the seat beside her, his leg stiffened out into the aisle. Some passengers, who had ridden the bus every evening for as many years as she had, nodded at her and glanced at him, examining him, she knew, for any resemblance to her, for only a relative would ride home with her after all her years of riding alone. Never out of the clear sky, out of the sky from where mates fell, would a sort of handsome man fall into the seat beside her, Naomi, the woman with a face flat and familiar as the advertisement placards above the bus seats.

"This knee is a good thing," he said. "I don't have to get up to let a lady sit down. You see?" His breath smelled of clove gum or mouthwash. His hand, gripping the horizontal steel rod on the back of the seat ahead, was a pale hand with high blue veins, almost the hand of a convalescent, but so strong in its power over her that she had to glance away. She felt sick with the suspicion that he was playing a trick on her. Only a drunk, only a man without a conscience could play a trick like this on a homely woman.

"You think I'm mean, Naomi, because I don't let a woman sit down?"

It was her chance to say yes. Yes, get up and get off and let somebody else sit down, somebody I'm used to. The only other answer she could give was No, and, by saying No, imply that she liked him sitting there, but if she said No, he'd go back to the bar and tell the bartender about what the scared, silly woman had said, that she liked him sitting by her.

"But I ain't a mean person, Naomi." He spoke so low the passengers in the seat ahead, their ears protruding to catch the conversation, could not hear. "Only I don't like to *prove* I ain't mean by doing something nice. When I have to do something nice, I feel mean." He gave a small, hiccuping laugh to tell her he was only joking. "Naomi sounds like an Indian name," he said. "There used to be a burlesque queen who was a full-blooded Cherokee. Some of them Indian girls are real beauties."

"Was that Princess Nadja?"

"Was who Princess Nadja?"

"The Cherokee girl."

"Hell, Nadja ain't an Indian name. It's Roosian, ain't it?"

"I thought you were married to the Cherokee queen."

"Me? I wasn't married to no Cherokee." He glanced up quickly as a few passengers, wanting out, pressed past the others standing in the aisle, and, when the commotion was over, he continued to gaze up into the faces above him. After a few moments, he suddenly sat up straight. "Three times," he said. "I been married three times, all of them fine women to begin with. I must of been fine to begin with myself or they wouldn't of begun with me." He laughed soundlessly. "There's a beginning and there's an end. Nobody likes endings and that's why they get bogged down in the middle."

"Which one was Princess Nadja?" she asked. That voluptuous woman with moon-white hair had become a terrible adversary, a woman whose seductiveness was as beyond her as the moon was beyond her. "I bet you made her up," she said, wanting to wound him, wanting to let him know she was not a dupe. "Am I right?"

"Right as rain," he said.

So she destroyed his imaginary princess, and the real ones remained beyond him, this pale, thin barker, pants presser, barman, clown. If she lived alone, she thought, she'd ask him in for supper. She would have no fear that he had come to sponge on her for a meal

and then make fun of her afterwards to the bartender.
She'd have no fear because she would say right off,
tough like Athena, You want to come in for supper?
You look like you need some meat on your bones.

He was smiling, maybe over the loss of Princess
Nadja, running his hand over his head, scratching
at the gray hair that had a mealy look though all his
clothes were clean as a whistle, scratching with a mon-
key's musing curiosity.

"I get off here," she said rising.

"Hey, hey," he said, confused, rising with her, hop-
ping out into the aisle, glancing toward the front of
the bus and toward the back, like someone trapped. A
string of hair swung out over his forehead as he swung
his head from left to right, and she bent her head into
his back, laughing at him. She poked her finger in between his shoulder blades to tell him he was blocking
her way. At once he lurched down the aisle, jerked forward and backward by the motion of the bus. Tossed
out, they stood on the corner before the drugstore's
lighted window confronting them with a jumble of
hot-water bottles, perfumes, toothpaste tubes, dead
flies, and holly wreaths.

Past stucco houses, mottled and faded like the one
she was going to, he walked beside her, fast, his narrow shoulders hunched under his rakish sport jacket.
It was a cold twilight with a rose-colored light in the
sky. "I can't come in," he said. "I got to get back and
meet this friend of mine at Rich's Cafeteria. I'm just
escorting you home because you're afraid of the dark."

After a block of the same houses, he asked her if she lived alone, and then he asked her who she lived with, and then if she had brothers and sisters, and, without any warning to herself to not tell, she was telling him about Hal.

"That's something I'd never do," he said, his voice mingling awe and pity. His small feet in polished old shoes, once stylish, went quickly, dapperly along. "I guess it takes courage, uh? Maybe I ain't got that kind of courage."

Was he praising her brother to ingratiate himself? But she wanted no member of her family around, least of all her dead brother. A man was walking her home. She had laughed with him on the jolting bus, she had been smart enough to see that he talked big, and cruel enough to tell him that she saw. Oh, what a fascinating life she led! The pleasure she had found in this encounter began to desert her now as she heard his praise for her brother, for her brother who was always praised, and praised now for the courage to take his own life.

"Well, so long," he said, the instant she paused by the small lawn worn bare in spots by children's feet. "Naomi sounds like a river," he said, and sang softly, *"By the banks of the Naomi, an Indian maiden waits for me.* You think that's a tune that'll catch on? You got a piano?"

"Yes," she said. "We used to play it but nobody's touched it for years."

"We'll work out a tune," he said. "We'll make a million bucks," and he gave a tricky salute, tugging at the brim of an imaginary hat, and went back the way they had come, a man wanting her to feel the loss of him. She could tell that much by the way he walked, briskly, confident of his charm.

That was the way it began. He rode home with her again and made excuses for not coming in before she made excuses for asking him in. He bought her lunch and invited her to a movie. After the movie she went up to his room in the National Hotel and he sat on his bed and she sat in the chair, and he told her about his other marriages. His first wife had died, his second had left him for another man, and his third he had left, and there was no Princess Nadja among them. The serious way he told about his life showed his respect for her. He percolated coffee on a hot plate and gave her some stale cookies to dip. On the sidewalk before her house he kissed her very lightly. The next time she went out with him they did not go to a movie. He met her in the hotel's drab, cold lobby and they went up to his room, and he was gentle in his passion. A delight began to stir in the core of her being, that night. It did not take her by surprise because she had suspected all along that it was waiting there.

Naomi was deserting her mother to go and live with a man who came out of nowhere. That was the way her mother described the change in the daughter. Naomi and her Dan were married by a judge in the county courthouse and moved into a rented duplex, and Naomi interviewed a woman for the job of companion to her mother. Mrs. Wade came into the recorder's office at noon, a plump, uneasy woman who couldn't smile, and Naomi became at once the one to be interviewed, reversing the positions, wanting not to subject the woman to the ordeal, the quivery-faced woman with the dodging eyes. They sat across from each other at the Dairy Lunch, and Naomi apologized for everything at home, the mix-up in the cupboards, the worn linoleum on the kitchen floor, and her mother's mind in captivity to her son's death. "You'll have to listen to all that," she said. "She's never going to give up her suspicions." Naomi told about everything that might displease the woman, wishing the woman would refuse the job now, because, if she walked out on the job later, she'd carry away with her a stranger's unsympathetic knowledge of secret sufferings, both Naomi's and her mother's.

The woman moved in that evening, and Naomi's mother called her at the recorder's office the next morning. *She doesn't answer me, Naomi. She was two hours in the bathroom last night. Nobody needs to take a bath that long. I was afraid she'd fainted. Suppose she died in there? She didn't answer me and finally I had to scream at her, and she said she's got a right to privacy.* Several nights later Mrs. Wade phoned Naomi at home. *Maybe you better come this one night. Maybe if she knows you come when I call you, she won't feel she needs you so bad. I been with old people like this before. One of 'em slashed his wrist so his daughter'd come back from New York. They think they can stop the sun from going down.* Naomi put on her coat and hat, left the supper dishes in the sink, and took a taxi to the house, and her mother clasped her in her thin arms. "She won't believe me," her mother complained. "I told her they did it to him, but she won't believe me."

It took a while before Naomi's mother and Mrs. Wade began to make balky, grudging moves toward one another, but when a kindly acceptance was found, the familiarity seemed too much for them to handle— what each one knew about the other. Then her mother began to call to her again.

"She went to her room right in the middle of cooking our supper and she won't come out," her mother said, waiting at the table in the kitchen, wearing the quilted satin bathrobe, a present from Cort and Naomi, an extravagant present to impress upon her their love that they knew would never, never compensate for the loss of her son, Hal.

"It's Naomi," she said, knocking at the door of the bedroom that had been her brothers' and then hers and was now Mrs. Wade's.

The woman opened the door after a minute, a quivery-cheeked woman with all her excess flesh that was too much of herself when the self was only a companion to a shrill old woman as deserted as herself.

The woman's pale blue eyes were enclosed in pom-poms of flesh, but, hidden as they were, they still attempted to slide away.

"Mama's sorry," Naomi said. *Ah, poor woman I ought to know!* she thought. And she was ashamed that she was only Naomi who was to be as deserted soon as this woman in the faded dress and the new apron. *Ah, poor woman! So much like myself and so much like Mama. We are all so much alike, skinny from loneliness or bloated with it.*

After that night, Naomi went across the city though nobody called her and though, often, she found her mother and Mrs. Wade contentedly, querulously watching the brawls and commotions on the television screen. She went because her husband was away in the bars until they closed, and because the nights he stayed home and drank alone, he played cruel jokes on her with words, jokes that ridiculed them both, himself and Naomi, *Na-o-mi,* the greenhorn, the goody-goody, the simple-minded woman who had fallen for him. Naomi sat beside her mother, holding her mother's hand, watching the screen and not remembering much from one second to the next, her soothing fingers sometimes pressing too hard on the bones of the hand she held.

One night he barred her way. "What're you putting your coat on for?" he said. "You ain't going anywhere." He was wonderingly sober.

"I'm going over to Mama's."

"You ain't going to Mama's, girlie," he said, and for a moment, because she was locked in and didn't know the man, she was a child again, her mind was a child's mind, wondering whether *girlie* was an affectionate word or a derisive one. Then she turned and ran down the hall to the back door. He ran after her and caught hold of her coat and threw her down on the kitchen floor. Her hip struck the floor and her face struck the table leg. She pulled her skirt down—it had leaped up past her knees—and attempted no other move, afraid that any move other than the modest one would make him more angry. For a second, as she lay stunned, she felt that he was right, throwing her down. It was such an extreme act, he must be right. Ashamed because she had brought him to violence, she could not look up into his face, she could only stare at his shoes. The great number of times she had left this apartment to find a queasy comfort from her comforting of her mother all added up to a crime. Her coming and going was a crime of futility.

"You're a goddamn saint, Naomi," he said, "but I ain't religious. It makes me sick to see a saint. They don't serve no good example, they just make you feel like a louse. Get up, get up," he said, banging around the coffee pot from one burner to another. The match he struck leaped out of his hand and fell on the table, and he swung after it furiously, and blew it out. With shaking hand, he struck another match. "Get up, get up. Sit down, sit down. Take off your coat, stay awhile."

She reached up to the table and drew herself up, and she sat down. Although she was suffocatingly hot, she left her coat on.

"Fix you some hot coffee," he said. "You should of seen all the coffee we drank over in England, on those cold nights with the V-1's buzzing around. Did I ever tell you about the time the anti-aircraft brought down a V-1 over the airfield? It began to bob around up there, turned around, changed its mind, and fell just half a mile away." He cleared his throat, a loud, raspy, prolonged scraping.

She was afraid to touch her cheekbone and afraid to lay her head in her hand, afraid that any soothing of herself might be mistaken for reproach.

"You going to take your coat off?"

She shook her head. The coat comforted her, the coat gave her dignity, it gave her access to the outdoors and protection against the inside of strange houses, like this one. She was about to draw her coat together when he went down on his knees, encircling her hips, laying his face in her lap, kissing the triangle into her closed thighs.

"Naomi, I wish I was a saint myself. Then it would be impossible for me to be mean."

"Danny, I'm no saint, Danny."

"Yeah, you are, you are, and when I leave that's what's going to make it easier for me because I'm going to say to myself, she's a saint and she knows I'm just human. You see what your trouble is, you saints? You make it easier for us to be human because you make allowances. Am I right? You make allowances?"

"I don't know what you mean."

"All I mean is you forgive people." He laid her hand on the crown of his head, moving her hand back and forth, and, when he took his hand away from hers, she went on stroking his head, thought she felt no love for this man who had come out of nowhere, out of everywhere, and fooled her into thinking she was his woman and fooled her again by elevating her above everybody else, calling her a saint because he was going to leave her and saints always forgive.

"Suppose you lived in Omaha, suppose you had children, suppose you died—your Mama would get along. She lost her precious son, so she's taking it out on you. Because you're just Naomi. What's Naomi doing, still alive? You ever stop to think that over? You ever stop to think?"

You ever stop to think? Stop *what* to think? The heart?

"When are you going?"

"Did I say I was going anywhere?"

"You said you were going."

"Oh, hell, I say that all the time. It keeps me alive."

Wiping her face with the sleeve of her coat, she stood up. She went down the hall to their bedroom and lay down on the bed, still with her coat on, face up. He followed her, sat down by the bed, and removed her shoes, chuckling, attempting his old seductive wit in the sound of it. "I bet you don't believe I ain't mad," he said. "That's a fine thing—you knock a woman down and then you tell her you ain't mad."

She lay weeping openly, uncaring how grotesque her face must be. She knew why he had pushed her down. He had pushed her down, this simple-minded woman, because she had turned her face toward him as toward the sun. Who had ever seen before that Naomi Costigan was a woman with a heart in her breast? He had pushed her down because she had made a mistake, because he was only a pale and shaky itinerant drunk, and she ought to have known. She ought to have known even from the start, even from the nights of love, and at last his contempt for her for not knowing threw her to the floor.

"Don't cry, Naomi," he said, kissing the soles of her feet. "I'm not going, don't cry."

So small his allotment of love! It seemed to her that each person at birth was granted an allotment of love to give to someone, or to two, or to three, or to the world, but how small his allotment of love! She didn't know how to measure other persons' love for her, like her mother's, like Cort's, but this man's was like Hal's. Her brother ran out on everybody, and this man was running out. They had the least to give. The least. Humbly, he was massaging her feet, his hands small and cold and straining to be of help, but her feet were numb to his hands, and her ears were deaf to his voice. She was transforming him into nothing, so that when he was gone no one would be missing.

8

Dolores returned to her parents' house four years after she had left it. When she climbed down from the bus, her father, waiting in the alleyway where the buses came in, embraced her. "Don't look at me," she said.

"Hell," he said, walking her solicitously to his car, arm around her, "you look like you ate too many kumquats. You took sick from kumquats when you were a kid."

The bedroom off the kitchen was waiting for her, curtains, spread, rug all new, all blue, a color she had turned against, along with ruffles. She took off her clothes that were saturated with the bus fumes and the sweat of her illness, slipped on a nightgown, lay down, and slept at once, slept on an immense airy bed of relief and return, wakened over and over by tormenting dreams.

At seven, her mother came home and into the bedroom on the soundless rubber-soled oxfords she wore at work. Dolores had seen her parents several times in

the years she had been away, when they had come up
to the city to visit her, but her mother's face, this time,
was glaringly older. The fever must be doing crazy
things to her eyes. Her mother bent over her, covering
her face with kisses. "It's all right, I'm immune," her
mother said. "Bugs run the other way."

For weeks she lay in bed, waiting for recovery.
Evenings, she watched her parents in the kitchen, an
audience of one observing two actors on the stage.
They had lived in marriage for twenty-five years and if
someone were to ask them to sing just one note, each
choosing one, they would sing the same note, she was
sure. The girl in the bed denied any accomplishment
in their similarity. Two persons, almost fifty years old,
who had never lived in any other city, who had never
held other lovers in their arms, what did they know?
Something more than she knew, or less? One afternoon, sleeping, she heard the vast silence in which the
neighborhood was set. Not since those last moments
between herself and the man in the shack on the beach
had she been surrounded by so much meaningful silence, and she listened for the breaking of the wave.
But this silence belonged to a time farther back, this
was the silence that surrounded Hal Costigan. Calling
for her mother, she woke herself completely to the fact
that it was early afternoon in her parents' house with
nobody home yet.

When she began to recover, she took short walks
to the drugstore and looked into the magazines, and
she sat in the shade of the trees in the backyard and

knit a sweater for her father, and she planted flowers, day by day, gradually, and when she felt strong enough, a girlfriend got her a job in a cocktail bar, working two hours on weekend evenings. She had her hair cut and curled and tinted red. She wore her filmy blouses and cinched her wide gold-leather belt tight around her waist. After a few weekends of parrying with the customers, she began an affair with a man older than herself and married, like most of the other men she'd been with. She went to meet him in vacant apartments and houses that he, as realtor, was agent for. He was big—football-player size—and that size, along with his deep blue eyes edged by thick black lashes, impressed the women shopping for homes with their husbands. His office chalked up more sales than any other in town, he told her.

Because she knew the affair would end, she began to imagine herself desperately in love with him. As always, there had to be some meaning to the time with a man. The meaninglessness of each time was like a sin for which there was no name. She repeated to him his criticism of his wife, and her caresses were promises to be the wife he ought to have. She held to him on mattresses that he covered with an old, faded spread he kept in his car, and begged him to love her.

On the day that was to be the last day, he was already in the apartment when she arrived. He was at the table in the dining room, reading the evening paper, his coat off, his feet up on a chair. He did not greet her. He was concentrating on something in the news

and on the secret use he was going to make of it. She
went into the bathroom to see again how her hair was
done, cut again and curled again and tinted red again,
and the sight of herself in the mirror evoked the many
mirrors in the beauty salon, where she had just been,
and all the reflected faces, hers among them, seemed,
in memory, like participants in a plot that would net
them nothing. She went into the kitchen to open the
cartons he'd brought.

"You ever see such stupidity?" he called. "God! If
you can't do it yourself, then don't do it at all. Here
the guy hires a two-bit gangster to do the job for him
and not only does he fumble it, he's a witness against
him, he sits up there and says Dr. Dick hired me to do
it. So it's just like hiring a witness against you, that's
what it comes down to." He read on for a minute.
"What's crazy about the whole thing is this—here the
guy wants to do away with his wife so he won't have to
give her half his fortune when he gets a divorce, and
now, boy, he won't have a penny left if he goes free. The
lawyers'll get it all. That's what I should have been, a
criminal attorney, get hired by all the guys who murder their wives." He had a loud, easy laugh that came
from down in his chest.

She spooned the delicatessen food onto the paper
plates, not answering. His ridicule of the man on trial
was another way, a final way, of telling her how impossible it was for a man to free himself of a vengeful wife.

"What's the matter? You sore at me?" he asked.

While they ate, he talked on about the trial. He

took his time when he ate, chewing with his big jaw, his mouth closed as his parents had taught him, his blue eyes pleased with the food and with the details of the trial that he was relating between the long, slow bouts of chewing. Over the coffee and cake, he said, "If you had in mind to do something like that, you couldn't ask your wife for a divorce because it would cast suspicion on you. If I'd ask Laurie, she'd tell her mother, she'd tell all her friends, she'd tell her auntie. The best way is to be lovey-dovey, the best way is to leave off seeing the girl for, say, two, three months, maybe a year, get close to your wife again. . . ."

"Go back to her!" she screamed. "You never left her so it won't be so goddamn hard to crawl into her bed again." With the back of her hand she knocked her empty paper cup off the table.

"The tenants," he cautioned.

"Everybody's stunted! Your Dr. Dick is stunted and his mistress is stunted and even the poor wife who got done in because she wanted all she could get, she was stunted, and the goddamn judge who has to sit there and judge, he's stunted, and all the jurors. Everybody is."

"Everybody is," he said, agreeably.

Lying beside him on the bed, knowing that this was the last time, she told him about Hal Costigan. She said that the man had been in love with her and had killed himself because of the scandal. She said that she was seventeen then and beautiful, as if she were old now, a remark to remind him that she was as beautiful now as ever and young enough to be his daughter. Voice breaking, she told the story into his ear, and she knew by the tension in his body that he was listening differently from the man in the beach shack. He was lying on his back, gazing up at the ceiling, listening closely, and when he turned to her she knew that she was as exciting for him as she had been their first night. The shame she felt over her version of the tragic, unknowable story of another man's suicide was effaced by the flaring up of her desire for this one.

When she left, he was sleeping so heavily he seemed to be sleeping away the density of his body, an infinitesimal amount with each exhalation. She covered him with the side of the spread that she had been lying on. The room was warm, the wall heater was on, but she could not leave him exposed in his nakedness. She put on her clothes, and, when she closed the door, she tried the knob over and over to make certain it was locked.

The apartments opened onto a small square court paved with dark red Mexican tile, spikey cactus plants in the corners. She went on tiptoe across the court, her high heels ringing only now and then on the tiles, and walked along the dark street toward her own neighborhood a mile away. On this street with its few dim lamps and overgrown shrubbery, she was back in the city of her childhood. She felt her return more than she had felt it on the day she lay down again in her own bed in her parents' house, because now Hal Costigan was close beside her again. She had called him up, back on the mattress, to make use of him in the living present, and here he was, beside her again and of no use to her at all. What he had done to himself made her all or made her nothing, and she had clung to the belief that it had made her all, because the other belief was unbearable—*to be nothing, to be nothing*. What he had done to himself told her she was nothing and everybody nothing and the world nothing.

A need to be consoled by her parents grew stronger the closer she came to their home. Her suspicions about her parents, about monotony, about each one's loss in the hope of gain, were blotted out by her need to be consoled. The door was left unlocked, sometimes, and tonight she saw a meaning in that negligence. It was natural, strangely natural, to live without fear of harm or loss. She went on to their bedroom, turning on no lights along the way, and paused in the doorway, calling softly to her mother.

"What? Dolores?" her mother called, sitting up.

She fell to her knees by the bed and took her mother in her arms, and her father sat up and switched on the lamp above them.

"Nothing's the matter," she assured them because everything was the matter but no one thing could be named.

9

The evening of the day her mother died, Naomi went for comfort to her brother Cort's house, knowing that no comfort was to be found there. She sat in the living room, she sat in the kitchen, she sat in the boys' room and read to them as they lay in crib and bed, she ate a small supper and drank several cups of coffee and talked with her brother and his wife, but found no comfort. Pauline was downcast and uncomfortable because she had disliked the old woman, Naomi knew, and must be feeling guilty now. Naomi saw the girl as the stranger of five years ago, and the small, forgotten discords of the girl's physical self were apparent again, like Pauline's sunken cheeks at odds with her large, round breasts. Everything, that day, was without a reason and in no need of a reason. Naomi sat on the sofa next to Pauline, and, as the girl bent forward to pour more coffee into the cups on the low table, she wondered if it were dampness that was causing the girl's fingers to curl back at the tips. Was dampness a sign of life? Like the blood, sweat, and tears Churchill had called for during the war? The pockets of Naomi's jacket were stuffed with damp tissues. The boys had come out from the bath wet, leaving wet tracks, dragging wet towels. All day she had sipped tea and coffee, and wept because her mother had grappled with life and it was like grappling with water.

"Yeah, she had a hard life," Cort said, over in the heavy chair. His face was long with sorrow and he couldn't look anybody in the eyes.

That's true and yet it isn't, Naomi thought. She had reminded herself during this day that there were millions of people who spent half their lives in prisons, in the places for the insane, there were men and women and children mutilated by bombings and those mutilated in their souls by cruelties, and that, back in the Depression, before the war, the hungry roamed the streets of every city, and in Europe a death corps rounded up thousands in one night. It might be impossible, she thought, to compare one person's pain with somebody else's.

"Yeah," Naomi agreed, obligingly pondering his remark. "She sure did."

"She had more than her share."

"Yeah, she had more than her share," Naomi agreed, though she didn't know what a share was, how much it was, and why there should be suffering like a law and a sharing of it.

"She expected a lot from Hal," Cort said, his legs stretched out far, elbows close, peering into the aperture that his curled hands formed close to his eye while the other eye was kept shut.

"Yeah, that was the worst thing."

"Jesus," he said, shifting in his chair, his long, thin body jerking with sudden anger. "Then that guy you married! Jesus, you could've picked somebody decent, Naomi."

Her laugh shot up out of her throat and collapsed. "When you get as old as me," she began, twisting her shoulders like a senile coquette.

"Oh, hell," he said. "You're not old. It's just you don't have much experience with men, and the first one who lays his hand on your knee . . ."

The restraints upon sorrowing were too harsh. The shamelessly loud cries she wanted to release would serve as her defense of her husband. They'd combine her sorrow over the loss of him and her mother. But another laugh shot out. "Yeah, that's the way it was. He put his hand on my knee and old stupid Naomi thinks this is it, this is it." She blew her nose.

Pauline's long, agitated fingers pushed strands of hair behind her ears. "Oh, he wasn't that bad," she said, embarrassed by her ambivalence toward Naomi.

The boy in his crib began to cry, a sudden waking-up crying.

"You want to see if you can shut that kid up, or shall I go?" Cort asked his wife.

"Let me go," Naomi said, rising. "I'll tell them goodnight again. Then I got to be running along." With pinching fingers she jerked her skirt straight.

"You got a nice shape, Naomi," he said. "You always did."

"Oh yeah, old knock-em-dead Naomi."

The older boy began to call for his mother to quiet his crying brother.

"You tell them both to shut up," said Pauline, generously giving over to Naomi some authority to wield.

Naomi found the older boy sitting up in his bed and the younger one sitting up in his crib, and in the sudden light from the hallway they quieted down, waiting to be told to be quiet. She hadn't wanted to come in here again, this blue room with its pile of dirty clothes, broken toys, and the humid ammonia smell of diapers. She knew that when they were to be her age she would mean nothing to them, only a speck of an aunt in the past. "Your Aunt Naomi wants to kiss you again. She's going now." Clowning, she gave them loud, smacking kisses.

"You want me to drive you home?" Cort asked her in the hallway.

"You stay right here," she said. "It'll do me good to sit in a bus. People around."

He followed her as she gathered up her coat and hat and gloves and purse, and helped her with her coat, docile, considerate, because he had wounded her. Pauline kissed her on the cheek. Naomi had always felt intimidated by this young woman, by her uneasiness, even by her tallness. Isobel, Hal's wife, had also intimidated her, but Isobel had done it with her prim, schoolteacher ways, and most of all by being

Hal's wife. They turned on the porch light for her. She stepped around a toy on the path, wondering crazily why the toy, left where someone could stumble over it, showed their disrespect for her mother's memory.

She sat at the back of the empty bus, and when she got off at the corner where she was to transfer to another bus, she went into a bar instead. In the bar's glowing, watery, slowly swirling colors, she might find what her mother had told her she would never find and that she needed now when her mother was dead—comforting from strangers. A small table by the entrance was empty, and she sat down and gave her order to the waitress, a woman her own age, with bleached hair and dangling earrings. She sipped her drink and felt the warmth spread down to her toes. The music on the jukebox vibrated along the floor. She gazed up at the hanging lamp that was like a metal ostrich egg pricked by holes through which the globe within shot out stings of light. She thought of how the life in her mother had sunk down and away, and fear of this sinking made her hand so shaky she almost knocked over her glass. She drank down the rest in a hurry because its effect was a rich swelling of life in her face and breasts and belly. She was filled now with her own presence, herself, whose eyes must resemble the lamp with the stings of light.

The man's face was at a discreet distance, but its smile brought it as close as a breath touching her face. Something was wrong with his face. The dark eyes were set too deep and one chunky cheek was lopsided, but there was a kindness in his face, elusive but there for sure. "You mind if I sit here?"

She waved him down. "You sure can."

"You crying for your mother?" He set his glass before him.

"How do you know?"

"The waitress told me."

She remembered the waitress's solicitous question, but she hadn't guessed that her answer would be relayed to somebody else.

"What'd she die of?" The slight Mexican accent, the quick, jerky voice—were they tricks to hide his indifference?

"You don't know a person, why do you want to know what they died of?"

"I'm sorry I asked," he said. "A person shouldn't ask. You're right."

She let him buy her another drink. He told her his name was Victor and that he was born in Texas, and he wanted her to guess how old he was. She squinted, guessing thirty-six. He slapped the table. "That comes of hard living," he said. "That comes of lifting sacks of potatoes up in Idaho, comes of being in the army, comes of digging ditches. I'm twenty-seven."

"You're younger than my kid brother."

"Don't treat me like a kid brother," he said, warningly. "I didn't sit down here to get treated like a kid brother."

She listened closely for signs of trickery in the blurry accent, and she examined closely his sidewards face and the shimmery, silvery stripes in his shirt, wanting to find him reliable despite the evidence against him. When they finished their drinks she went out with him into the street, and he put his arm around her and his hand into her armpit, implying that she had to be held up because of her sorrow.

"Have you got sisters and brothers?" she asked.

"I got a kid brother in the army. I got a sister, too. Fifteen."

"Three kids in the family?"

"Yeah," he said.

"That's like us."

"That's a coincidence, uh?"

"Except one of us is dead," she said.

He said nothing, showing no interest in the missing one.

"My brother," she said. "Not the kid brother I was telling you about, but my other brother."

"That's terrible," he said, his voice jerky with desire.

"He was going to be President of the United States," she said.

"Ahhh," he said, exhaling sympathy.

"I could've been sister of the President. They would've given me a filing job in Washington, D.C., for three times as much as I make now. That's the way you do things, you elevate your family and all your relations. I would've been elevated."

"It's too bad he died," he said, giving her a deft

push in the small of her back, guiding her toward a doorway.

She began to climb a flight of stairs to a hallway of doors that she saw above. Behind her on the narrow stairs, he lifted up her coat at the back, but before his hand touched her she backed against the wall.

"You know what he did, I'll tell you," she said. Her purse slipped out from under her arm as she lifted her hands to shield her breasts from his heavy face. "You know what he did? He killed himself. Now there's nothing as bad as that, is there? That's what he did to his own mother. He threw his life right back at her."

"Come on, come on," he urged, picking up her purse and swatting her hip with it to make her turn and go up.

"That's what he did to Mama," she said, climbing.

At the top, she was assailed by the picture of her mother waiting at home for the wayward daughter to return sometime in the night, waiting for the daughter who was her bosom friend, her dear slave, waiting in a cold, dark house for the daughter who wasn't coming home this night. The mother would have to stay alone this night because the daughter wasn't fit to come home.

10

On his last day with the company, Cort Costigan came home after work, bringing another employee who had also been weeded out, and two six-packs of beer. He brought the man, who had been barely more than an acquaintance, because the other's presence reminded him that he was not the only one fired, and he wanted his wife to be reminded of it. Pauline was sitting on the front steps in the sun, absorbing sun into her long body for the benefit of the child within her. When both cars drew to the curb she watched, unwelcoming. Cort saw, from afar, her rebuff of the visitor. She must have wanted him to come home alone on this last day of his job, wanting no spectator. She spoke sharply to the kids playing in the water sprinkler on the lawn, and by the time he and the intruder had come up the walk, she had already grabbed up the younger boy and was tugging up his wet shorts, scolding him because she couldn't scold Cort.

Cort introduced the fellow, who was so shy he

seemed to bend away from her. They stepped past her and the boy and went through the house to the kitchen. Cort opened two beers, and the intruder sat down only after Cort sat down, and then with a joke and a mumble. Sprawling in his chair to persuade the intruder to feel at home, Cort wondered why the man's timidity had never been so evident around the insurance office. The loss of his job and the unsmiling woman on the front steps must have caused him to collapse.

"Let's celebrate this promotion, boy," Cort said, and the intruder clutched at his chest, his laugh as painful as a heart attack.

They drank their beer and, in the midst of their first swallowing, began to laugh again. Cort heard his own laugh go high and wild as it used to when he was a boy. "You ever think old Snyder, you ever think old Snyder . . . ," bowing his head to the table, covering his nose to trap the snorts inside, "looks like a fish? Like one of those brute fishes, where their lower jaw comes up to their eyes? If you saw old Snyder lying among the other fish down at the Crystal Market, you wouldn't be surprised, would you?"

The intruder sputtered his beer. "I'd say slice that one for me!" pointing with his pale, stabbing finger that had no job.

"Ah, slice it!" Cort said.

"The girls . . . ," gasped the intruder.

"Go on!"

"The girls, specially Rosalind, the girls, all the girls in the whole goddamn claims department—bitches,

bitches! The only one I like is little Susie. She wrote me a note, hey, she wrote me a little note on her type-writer, says—here, read it—says, 'You are one of the nicest people at Fidelity. I hope you find a position you will enjoy.'" He clutched his face, spattering laughter through his fingers. "She's fresh out of high school, she doesn't know what she wrote. What I ought to do is write back, 'Dear Susie, the only position I will enjoy is one with you under me.' Oh, great!"

"You know that machine they got that chews up the old records, old stuff they don't want around any-more? Hell, take the whole damn Fidelity building, take the lunchtime movies, take the roof garden, take the girls and the boys, take 'em all, the long and the short and the tall, take their Fidelity Frolics, run 'em through the masticator, maserator, what's it called?"

"Don't let the efficiency man get away! Anybody who'd train himself for a job like that is queer as an undertaker, queer as a queer," said the intruder.

Cort leaned his chair far back. Once he'd gone over in the shaky metal chair, and, afraid it might embar-rass him again, he held to the table's edge with his fin-gertips. "They had their eyes on me," he said. "Snyder says to me, 'You happy here, Costigan?' I thought he was kidding. I thought, 'You tell *me*, boy. You want me to go around kissing ass?'"

"You're not a smiler."

"But that doesn't mean I was unhappy, man!"

"You never looked unhappier than anybody else. Snyder—he look happy to you?"

"Snyder's the saddest sack this side of . . ." The spindly legs of the chair were slipping away and he gripped the table. "Hell, I'm glad I'm through with the bastards. I think I'll go back to selling refrigerators. Get to walk around. I always felt like a fairy, sitting at a desk. My calf muscles are down to nothing. Lost my elasticity. I'm like an old rubber band—can't snap anymore." He heard a child's footsteps in the living room, and waited. His younger son appeared in the doorway, red shorts wet, face impassive. "You want some little thing?"

Pauline came up behind the boy. "He can have milk and a cracker. It's too close to dinner." Because her words were an inescapable hint to the intruder, she kept her eyes down as she crossed to the refrigerator.

"I guess I'll be going," said the intruder.

"Finish your beer! Finish your beer!" Cort commanded. "We got a long ways to go before dinner. She says that so he doesn't spoil his appetite." He could ask the intruder to stay for dinner. He could do that in spite of his wife. But, pouring more beer, he admitted that he was eager to be rid of him. The man was a reminder of the company, and only after the fellow was gone would the severing be complete. They knew each other too well. At their desks they'd assumed their position of indebtedness, they'd joined in the exhibitive laughter, they'd kept their boredom from their eyes as if it were a crime, something stolen from the company, and now, worst of all, they were hilarious outcasts together. "What am I going to do with all this beer, man? You've got to help me get rid of it."

The child climbed onto a chair and watched the milk pouring into the glass, his fingers laid out flat on the table.

"How old are you?" the intruder asked. "Twenty-one?"

"You think we got a midget here?" Cort went off into his high laugh again.

"You a midget?"

The boy still gazed, forgetting his milk.

"Something funny about my face?" the intruder asked, covering it with his hands and staring back at the boy from between his fingers.

"You've got Fidelity branded on your forehead, man," Cort said. "You got it there as long as you live." He pointed to his own forehead. "See mine? Every place I ever worked got their name branded on me. That's the only way people got of knowing who you are, they read all those company names on you. The more names you got, the less they can trust you. Snyder's got only one name on his—Fidelity."

"Mighty Mouse Snyder," said the intruder.

They gagged on their laughs. The intruder controlled himself sooner than Cort because Cort's wife, unsmiling, was standing by the boy's chair, a long-legged woman in shorts with a pregnant belly, a composite condition that embarrassed the man unmercifully.

"Sit down and have a beer," Cort said to his wife.

She sat between him and the boy, her chin in her hand. Her sun-bleached hair hung in strings to her shoulders—she hadn't curled it for a long time—and her face was blotchy. Her throat was a little thick with the fat that always came with her pregnancies, but no fat ever came to fill out the hollow cheeks, and her eyes appeared lashless because the lashes were as light as her hair. Cort suspected her of retaliating against him by looking that way. He suspected that the only way she could retaliate against the company for firing him while she was pregnant with their third child, and retaliate against the pregnancy that went on for so long, was to retaliate against him, her husband, closest, handiest, and more imperiled than she had ever expected any man to be. He kneaded her shoulder affectionately, telling her, in that way, that she was the woman for him, and that it was her love for him, not her grimness, that was getting through to him.

The intruder was thrown into a state of confusion by this kneading. Cort's hand on his wife's bare shoulder insinuated their intimacy and its result. He shifted in his chair, crossing and recrossing his legs.

"Do you have another job lined up?" she asked him, her voice softer than her face.

"My wife's brother," he said. "My wife's brother's in auto supply, he's going to put me on the floor, selling."

"Your legs won't hold you up," Cort said. "They been bent too long."

The intruder gripped his thigh, massaging it involuntarily in the same way Cort massaged his wife's shoulder. "If I can find something else, I'll take that instead. For the reason that I hate my wife's brother.

He's got a knack for making me feel like . . ." For the obscene word in his mouth he substituted "a nobody. You ever meet anybody who made you feel like a nobody? You ought to meet him."

"That's just the kind of guy I shouldn't meet," Cort said.

The obnoxious brother-in-law became an enemy in common. They swallowed down more beer, knocked off the ashes of their cigarettes, while the intruder kept shaking his head over his relative, cursing in his cheek as if his anger were a fingernail he'd bitten off and wanted out of his mouth.

"Yeah," Cort said, clicking his index finger against his beer glass, "the world's full of bastards. It's a bastard world. Everybody wanting his, spitting in your eye, crossing off your name. If you don't like that stuff, if you don't like it, you might as well do yourself in because you're going to get done in anyway." In the midst of his tirade he heard the click of his nail repeated by his son on his own glass.

"You can say that again," the intruder said.

Cort saw his wife take down the child's hand to stop the tapping and hold it firmly under the table. The boy began to squirm and cry.

"That's what my brother did," he went on. "He said to hell with it."

Pauline lost to the boy's struggles and released his hand. The tapping on the glass began again, the child staring at the visitor, seeking praise of his talent.

"The man had a heart," Cort said, his voice rising.

"You're not supposed to have a heart, you're supposed to be ashamed of it, you're supposed to hide it or get rid of it, do something. But he couldn't help it, he had a heart." He narrowed his eyes, probing the visitor's eyes. "You around then?"

"When was it?"

"Six years ago," he said. "Come October."

"No," said the intruder. "I was in L.A. We came up here a year ago. My wife wanted to be near her sister. Then I got this job with Fidelity." He was giving details of his own existence to forestall details from Cort, and Cort, realizing how close to breaking he looked, dropped his gaze but let his story run on.

"He was what you'd call a complete man. You know what I mean? I mean he had everything. He was on his way up because he had a mind, he was smart. God, that man could persuade. But he had a heart, too. That was his trouble. He couldn't stand the dog eat dog. That's the only thing to do if you got a heart, man. Bow out. So he bowed out just before the curtain went up. He was running for Congress, see?"

The child continued to tap the glass, smiling.

"It's no place for a man with a heart," said the intruder solemnly, pushing the ashtray around with his knuckles.

Pauline took the boy's hands again and held them in a hard clamp, and the boy wailed and thrashed around in his chair.

"He's doing all right, leave him alone!" Cort told her, his voice high and breaking.

"That isn't the reason," she said.

"Then why're you holding his hands?"

"I'm talking about your brother. That isn't the reason." A corner of her mouth jerked down.

"You never even knew him!"

"People with hearts, they don't kill themselves. I know people with hearts. I can name you some."

"Name me some!" he shouted. "Name me some!"

The intruder laughed, embarrassed, responding to his host's challenge as to a joke.

"He was weak," she said.

"Oh, Jesus, it takes a hell of a lot of courage to do what he did."

"He was weak."

Cort put his fists to his temples. "What the hell do you know about it? What the hell do you know what goes on in a man?"

The child was crying under the table. He felt the soft body when he moved his feet.

"What I know is you talk too much about messes."

"That's what they are. You going to deny it?"

"No, I don't deny that," she cried. "All I'm saying is you don't have to kill yourself to show you don't want any part of it. All I'm saying is there's lots of people with hearts. They stay alive as long as they can."

He struck the table. "Don't tell me about your people with hearts. Anybody I'll name, it'll be somebody you don't like. You take my sister Naomi. You don't like her. There's somebody with a heart and you don't like her. You say she's a sap, she's a clown."

The boy was climbing up from the floor and she was trying to help him. Then, realizing that she was drawing him onto her lap when she did not want him there, she unclasped his hands from her clothes and held him away.

"Every time you get a friend in here," she was saying, "every time we go anywhere, you've got to bring up about your brother. You make death sound like something to brag about. You talk like death is all there is to life."

"He was my brother!" he shouted, stumbling up from his chair. She had never criticized him before about his brother, she had never complained. Why had she chosen the worst possible time, now in the presence of this loser, who would go on his way convinced that Cort Costigan was the real loser, a man with a monstrous habit, an attachment to a dead man.

The loser stumbled up with him. "I got to be going."

Cort walked him to the door, shook hands, said, "See you around," and closed the door. On his way back to his wife at the table he stopped in the kitchen doorway, his fists straining dangerously down at his sides. This anger, trapping him there, seemed not to be against his wife. Who, then? Who, then? But something was terribly wrong if this anger was against his brother. Unmercifully wrong. He made his way to the table, sat down by his wife, took her hand in both his hands, and lay his head down on the knot their hands made together.

11

Seagulls were flapping along after the ferry, hovering high and low on the wind. "Bigger than most birds, aren't they?" Naomi remarked to the waitress who was sliding the coffee toward her. "Oh, but ostriches, too! I forgot!" and laughed. "*They're* really big!" She gazed out the ferry windows again, her legs crossed, her high heel caught on the rung of the stool. They might not be as big as some, but they're bigger than the sparrows back home. Cold-eyed birds! What else could you expect, with cold, sea-salty crud in their gizzards, fishheads and guts and wet crusts of bread? She was smiling humoringly at them in case anybody was watching her. The whole city was cold, a gray puzzle beyond the windows, beyond the dipping, flapping, mean-eyed birds. The fish-gray water was cold and God knew how deep under this rumbling tub of a ferryboat. "Oh, they're strong birds all right. My, they got strong wings!" trilling her flattery, ducking her head to drink her coffee.

"You sure don't realize how big the world is, do you? No, you sure don't," she answered herself, and asked for a bearclaw to eat with her coffee. The more she purchased, the more the waitress might like her. She cut the pastry into four strips, picked up one daintily, and, with the avid, happy eyes of the enchanted visitor, watched the smoke-brown buildings slide by. The hotel room where she'd slept last night—all night long a bad smell kept waking her. Was it a mouse rotting? Or was it only her own fear of a strange city? "Can't make out which hotel is mine!" She laughed, half expecting the waitress to turn her head and help her find it. *You're over forty yourself,* she said to the waitress. *Is that why you can't smile? But you're in your own city, behind your own little counter on your own chuggling ferry, you chuggle along in the same watery groove every day. You're not far from home. You didn't spend last night in a dead-mouse hotel room.* Was it done in this city, too, like that woman had done a year ago back home, checking into a hotel and the next day found on the bed, dead from an overdose of sleeping pills? What the hell you trying to do? she asked herself. Stir up this woman's sympathy with a threat of what you'll do to yourself if she doesn't smile at you? She can't read your mind, she can't even read your face.

The stale pastry was like a wad of paper in her mouth. She washed it down with the coffee and glanced contentedly around. They keep these ferries clean all right, she thought. Windows clean as sky, long benches varnished with a thick, dark wine of a shine, floors mopped. Over by the door of the ladies' lavatory, two men in white overalls were painting light green paint over the old-fashioned dark green, each man down on a knee, each painting with slow and easy, careful strokes. Everything shipshape, engines rumbling along, hot coffee in the urn, candy machine and popcorn machine standing against the wall like members of the crew. *My those ferryboats are a joy to ride!* That was the first thing she'd say to Isobel. *They keep them so clean!* she'd say, as if Isobel had a hand in it. *My, this part of the country, I bet you can't beat it. Why, Mount Rainier looks just like a dish of ice cream standing up there behind Seattle, and all those mountains, my, they make a pretty background for the city. Just like an oil painting!*

What a shock to the heart to see someone waiting for you who didn't want to be waiting! Isobel. Isobel, wife of her brother, Hal. Once they'd been friends— wife and sister. But in the six years since Isobel and her son had fled, there'd been only a card at Christmas, with that hasty blue-ink signature that said, *You're just one among many,* and the card not even to her, Naomi, only to her mother, with herself understood as sharing, and after her mother died, no cards. The city was far behind them now, most of the seagulls had flapped away, and far out across the gray water was the shore where Isobel waited.

"If you're getting off at Winslow, you'd better get up to the front," the waitress advised after the second cup of coffee. "You can see the ferry put into the slip."

One high-heeled shoe found the floor, her knees stretching her tight skirt. She dug out her coin purse to slip a quarter under the saucer. Pay her to make her like you, she thought, teetering a bit on the black suede heels of her red pumps, drawing her coat around her. Two men in dark suits, facing each other on the face-to-face, back-to-back benches, unrememberable men, reading newspapers, glanced up as she left her perch and glanced down again, uninterested in a woman with a homeless face, anxious eyes way in under painted black eyebrows, and dyed black hair in stiff, chic curls under a red hat. *It doesn't hurt so much any more, thanks,* she said to them. *The older I get the more used to it I get. When the time comes when you don't look up at all, then I won't feel anything.* She knelt to pick up her overnight case, and in that small activity, because they did not watch her, a feeling of immeasurable abandonment came over her. For several moments she could not rise. Clutching her coat together, she went forward toward the bow.

Now through the windows she saw land again, forested hills, narrow beaches with little cottages, sailboats moored to docks, and again the wash of waters against and over things, over broken docks, over logs on the sand, and the merciless rocking of everything on the waters. Close overhead, she saw a seagull borne back on the wind, saw the white breast, saw the light from the sky shining through the wings, saw the beak with the preying knob, saw the crazed eye. There was the slip, its high, slanting timbers rising up out of deep water, there the long black ramp up to the concrete building, and there, on that higher level, a parking lot with tiny cars far away and growing larger. Small figures wandered about up there. Which one was Isobel? But in that moment, seeking out Isobel and avoiding her, she felt the frightening closeness of her mother barring her way in a narrow hallway, Mama in the satin robe. *What've you come to see Isobel for? She never wrote, she never brought Hal's son back for me to see. What Hal did to himself, she's to blame because she was no wife to him.* Naomi put up her gloved hand as though to clear a spot on the window glass.

The engines changed their tune, or did they stop? The rumbling stopped, the ferry struck against a piling, and her hand at the glass helped her to keep her balance. A man in a uniform ran down the narrow iron ladder from the captain's cabin and disappeared around the deck. The cluster of passengers was increasing at the bow, the wind blowing up hair and scarves and coat hems. It must be like docking a big ship, she thought. You haven't come very far in forty-six years, she said to herself. *Isobel,* she begged, *forgive me for being a hick, for coming to visit. I won't stay long, I'll stay just tonight.* A child out on deck, his hand in his mother's, was gazing over his shoulder at her, and she changed her face to the face of a dazedly happy visitor awaited eagerly by someone up there in the town.

They embraced, kissing each other's cheek, each bending to pick up the overnight case and Isobel gripping it first. It was done as it ought to be done, for anybody watching and for themselves, and, arm in arm, they walked to the parking lot.

"If anybody'd asked me, I could have picked it out!" she said as Isobel unlocked the car door. "There's something so neat about it!" Not old, not new, a clean, light green sedan with plaid green seatcovers. "You were always such a neat one!"

"Guy's very cooperative," Isobel said, settling in the driver's seat, smoothing her coat under her, fitting the key with a sure hand. "He uses the car, too, mostly on weekends. Even though he takes his friends with him—they go to the beach or Seattle or Mount Rainier—why, he brings it back in good shape, even the ashtrays emptied."

Naomi doubled over with a disbelieving laugh. "Guy drive? Oh, God, I keep seeing a twelve-year-old boy. He's a man!"

"In September he'll be starting at the university," Isobel said, glancing over her shoulder as she reversed the car out of the line. "Medicine."

"Medicine? Oh, you mean he's going to be a doctor!" Again Naomi bent over, laughing, because she was so dense. She's still Isobel, she thought. She's got her own schoolteacher way of saying things, and she looks more like a teacher now than ever. So vapory kind, like a nun. "Well, isn't that nice! A doctor! There's nobody in the world gets more respect than a doctor."

The houses were far apart in this town. Back in her own neighborhood, they were boxy stuccos of pastel colors, plots of grass in front littered with children's toys and paper. They passed an acre of grass, two horses grazing, then a long row of small houses all alike, gray frame with dark green trim. "Company houses," said Isobel, and Naomi nodded as though she knew the meaning. Then, after more grass, "That one? The white one?" she asked, peering through the windshield, directed by Isobel's pointing finger. "Say, that's sure a cute little house."

"It belonged to my aunt," Isobel said. "She left it to me. She died three years ago. We've got awfully nice neighbors. Another teacher at the high school lives just a couple of houses down, the green one, see? And on the other side of us there's a nice family, he works on a newspaper in the city. They're all nice people around."

Isobel parked the car exactly before the few stone steps to the yard so that, in lieu of an honest welcome, there was a path for the guest's feet directly as the guest stepped out of the car. Naomi thought—Anybody looking out a window would see a smartly dressed visitor, nice figure, nice legs, nice posture, a visitor positive of her welcome, carrying a snappy, round, black and white overnight case. A forever-young woman delighted with small surprises. "Say, look what you got here!" pausing on the concrete path. "Clam shells! Say, don't they make a pretty border!" her voice the voice of Athena, a tough woman with a kind heart.

So this is the house Isobel got for herself! Naomi passed through the little hallway and into the living room, her heels muted by braided rugs. This is the

house where Isobel found refuge, protected by distance and silence. "Oh, say, this is cozy, Isobel!"

"Let me take your bag upstairs," Isobel said.
"You're welcome to my bedroom."

"No, no!" shaking her head vigorously. "What's
the matter with the sofa? I'll sleep on the sofa. Won't
be any trouble to anybody, that way," tossing the bag
onto the sofa, removing her hat, her coat, and tossing these over the bag. "Wait'll I get my cigarettes,"
she called after Isobel who was moving on into the
kitchen to make tea, and, fishing up the package from
her purse, holding it under her breasts, she followed
Isobel. At the kitchen table, she hung a cigarette on
her lips and struck a match. "I can stay overnight, like
I told you, but I got to get back in the morning. I'm
staying with friends in Seattle and it wouldn't be po-
lite if I stayed away longer. They drove me to the ferry
and I wanted them to come along for the ride, but they
said it's nothing new to them. Real nice people. The
wife used to work in the recorder's office with me."

She sat down, leaned back, flicking together the
nails of thumb and little finger to make a hard, worldly,
nervous clicking. "Say, you've got a sweet little kitchen
here!" glancing around at the crockery windmill clock
on the wall, at the crockery Dutch boy and girl with
ivy growing out of their heads, at the yellow and green
curtains with ruffles. "Nobody keeps house like Isobel,
that's what Mama always said. You remember?" Her face
lapsed. "Mama's dead, you know. I wrote you, didn't I?"

Isobel was setting teacups down, place mats,

teaspoons. "We were sorry to hear," she said. "And I thought to myself, wouldn't it be nice if Naomi could come here for a visit, a change of scenery. Last night when you phoned, we were so pleased. Guy said," and she laughed, "he said 'I wonder if she looks like I remember her, in a blue dress.'"

"Mama never did forgive you for taking Guy away," she said, thinking, Why am I making accusations for Mama? "I was always having to explain to her how I figured you felt. But you did do everything so fast, hustled him off on the plane, sent him all that way, a kid alone."

A slice of lemon slid off the saucer Isobel was setting down. She picked it up with hasty fingers. "The stewardess took care of him," her voice flat. "And my aunt met him in Seattle. He was twelve years old already."

"That's what I told Mama," her voice rising with dolorous insistence like that of a child who is seldom listened to. "That's what I said. Oh, I was always defending you, Izzybell. Remember how I used to call you Izzybell? Oh, say, I sure missed you, Izzybell."

Isobel sat down angrily, a teacher fed up with a student's perverse behavior. "One thing, one thing let me ask of you. Not one word to Guy about his father's suicide. Not one word. And for that matter, not to anybody else, if anybody comes by while you're here."

"Oh, God, never!" clasping her throat. "Never. What did you think, that I came all the way here just to bring up old troubles?"

"That's all I ask."

"Well, that's certainly not too much to ask." She

laughed. "You don't have to be afraid of me, that's just a little thing to ask."

Isobel pushed herself up as if already unbearably weary of this visitor, and, at the stove, pouring boiling water into the flowered teapot, her back to the visitor, she asked cheerily, "Tell me about *you*. Anything interesting?"

"Me?" Naomi crossed her legs, sliding her palms down along her thighs, and clasping her hands together when they met upon her knees. "I got married. Yes, I did. I was going to write and tell you, but oh, my, it was like the roof falling in. Dan, his name was Dan O'Leary, that's just what it was, and a nice guy, nice as pie, but an alcoholic. One of those real ones. It didn't last long, the marriage I mean, oh, maybe six months. He went back to New York, business stuff. He never wanted me to go and see Mama, I had to fight with him. When he left, I moved back with her." All told with a shrugging of shoulders, with pulls on her cigarette, and a crossing and recrossing of legs.

"What was his business?" Isobel asked.

"Oh, he used to be an engineer, really. He used to be a big time engineer, he was that smart. But then his alcohol craving got the better of him, and he started drifting."

"It's sad, isn't it, what it does?" Isobel, sipping her tea.

Naomi rubbed her knees. "You'd never believe your sister-in-law, old workhorse Naomi, you'd never think she'd start drinking around, now would you? I used to go around to the bars with him, got to like it.

Oh, don't get worried!" holding up her hand. "Don't worry about *me*. I'm off it now, haven't had a drink since the night I almost got run over. After Dan left and I moved back with Mama, I used to go out after she was asleep, go visit the bars. Up until the night I almost got it. That sobered me up."

"What about Cort? What's he doing?"

"Cort? Kid brother Cort? He was just twenty-six when you left, wasn't he? Well, now he's married, got himself a nice honey, and they got two boys, yep, two boys, and now they got a baby girl. They don't waste time these days, do they? The oldest boy's the smartest kid you ever saw, four years old and talks like a judge. Mama used to say he was going to grow up to be like his Uncle Hal. But Hal was one in a million. Everybody watching him. Watch that man going nowhere but up! Got out of law school, right away he's in with the biggest lawyer in town. If he'd made that election to Congress, I'll bet he'd be a Senator now. Senator Hal Costigan. It's okay, isn't it, if I tell Guy what a smart father he had?"

"He knows it."

"What did you tell him happened?" she asked, dartingly.

"I told him it was a heart attack."

"That's what *I'll* say, then. Because I've got to talk about Hal, you just can't not talk about him. You can't come and meet the son of a man like Hal and not say something about his father. That's asking too much."

"That's not what I asked."

"I know what you asked. You don't have to tell me twice," a friendly jabbing in her voice, a pretense at being offended.

At four, Guy came home. Naomi, rising, cried, "Look at that boy! It's Guy, I bet!" She stood on tip-toe to kiss him on both cheeks. "Your Mom said you remember your Aunt Naomi," holding his hands, swinging his arms from side to side.

"That's true," he said, trying not to lower his eyes, trying not to shift his feet.

"You sure don't look like your Dad!" roaming her gaze over his broad face, like Isobel's, over the ugly haircut, shorn close, glancing down to the large feet in hiker's boots. Looks like any other teenager, she thought. "Don't get me wrong, you're a good-looking guy, but you don't look like your Dad."

She dropped his hands, rattled by her own effusiveness. Slowed by her behavior, self-conscious, he took off his leather jacket and washed his hands at the kitchen sink. She helped set the table, laying out plates edged in blue and gold, lifting silverware from the wine velvet lining of the case, protesting that she wanted to eat on any old plate with just any old fork. The ornaments for the meal and the meal itself, composedly created by Isobel, an apron across her little bulge of a stomach and a glimmer of sweat on her brow, all were declarations of this guest's imposition. While they ate, Naomi told old family jokes, even joggling Isobel's foot for emphasis, but all the while aware of Guy's sullen face, given grudgingly to a smile. Catch Hal with a face like that when he was a boy, and he'd change quick as a flash. But this one showed it off, as if he'd made it all by himself. Maybe it was the time of life to be sullen, maybe it was natural, she thought. Maybe I wanted to be sullen, too, but Mama wouldn't let me. "You got a girlfriend? I bet you got a girlfriend."

"Up 'til yesterday," he said.

Oh-ho, there's the reason! she thought, as Isobel said, "And tomorrow there'll be another. Guy never has to worry."

"What're you talking about?" he demanded. "You said yourself that Alice was a prize, you said nobody, no other girl, measured up to her. Why do you make it sound so, oh, so damn, oh, like it doesn't matter?" Filling his mouth with peas, he deprived her of the chance to answer, as if it were her mouth he had stopped. His mother ate on neatly, implying that to observe pauses in conversation was an art.

Oh-ho! Naomi thought. His girl's thrown him over. That's why his eyes can't lift up, that's why he looks like a mean bear.

"Alice Ann is a nice girl, prettier than most, lots of personality," Isobel explained to Naomi. "Her father is a physician and her mother comes from a wealthy family, and Alice Ann has been, well, she has that manner of having the advantages."

What's she doing? Telling me that Guy deserves the best things in life? Naomi saw Guy's hands breaking a biscuit and buttering it, callow hands that had petted around the girl's prize body. Like a handshake with a movie star, maybe he'd never wash his hands again to keep the feel of the girl on them, and when he was married to some other girl and had three kids, he'd tell the fellows in the bar about that one who got away.

"They were going to be married," Isobel said. "Her parents like him so much. He was over there twice a week for supper. They were even going to help him with medical school. Then her brother comes back for the summer with this friend of his from Harvard, and the friend, well, he and Alice Ann, well, she fell in love with him. Yesterday she broke it off with Guy. She cried about it."

"All right, tell it all," he grumbled. "She cried. . . ."

"That's what you said!"

There he was, trying not to be pleased with the fact that she'd cried. At least she'd cried, he'd always have that to remember. Naomi ate on, daintily, a guest appreciative of every morsel and their sharing of family matters.

"She cried," he said. "So what?"

They ate on in silence. Naomi shifted in her chair, an involuntarily flirtatious move, flipped her napkin and spread it again over her lap, trying to quiet an odd triumph over his loss. "I guess I better not take seconds," she said, "because I saw that cherry pie."

"They're cherries from the tree in our yard," Isobel said, exaggerating their pride in that bountiful tree.

"Oh, I saw it!" Naomi cried. "Aren't you the lucky ones!"

* * *

When the kitchen was tidied, Naomi followed Isobel into the small garden at the front of the house, and while Isobel troweled around the plants, Naomi, in a borrowed sweater, wandered up and down the concrete path, arms crossed to keep herself warm. "The air here sure is different," she said. She gazed up into the branches of the cherry tree, every branch hung with a profusion of red and yellow cherries. The cherries were the colors of sunset, the colors of life and variety, the stems so springy, curving with the weight of the tiny fruit, the sky like large, pale blue leaves intermingling with the green leaves.

The trowel made a dry, rasping sound. She went over to Isobel's squatting figure, her shoes on the gravel between the flower beds sending up a fiery sound. "You mean Guy goes all the way to those mountains just for the snow?" hugging herself, facing the range across the waters and beyond the city, mountains almost transparent, almost air.

The trowel rasped on, clods broke apart. "You know, I never mentioned it to Guy, but there's something about Alice Ann I didn't like. She's calculating. She saw possibilities in Guy. She was the one who made the first move, she invited Guy to go on a hiking trip with her parents. But all the time I kept thinking—If somebody comes along who's a little older than Guy, say, knows more about women . . ."

Isobel unbent, rubbing her gravel-bitten knees on the way up, her trowel with its flakes of dirt held outward. "In a way, I'm glad it happened."

Don't bother me with her hot and cold, Naomi pleaded. *Because the only one I knew was Dan, and a couple more that were hotel-room romances. If I ever go up to a room again, I'll go up every night until I come into the courthouse some morning reeking with the smell of the man and me, and my stockings hanging down in baggy wrinkles, and after that I'll have to live in one of those rooms.* Cozily bowing her shoulders, she went ahead of Isobel to the door. "Say, this sure is a cute sweater. You knit this one yourself?"

Guy was on the hassock, watching television. When they entered the darkening room, he straightened up from his slump.

Naomi collapsed in the center of the sofa, stretching out her legs. "Say, it gets chizzly around here, doesn't it? What we could use right now is a little bitty rum or something."

Isobel knelt to light the oil stove. "We've got a bottle of brandy somewhere. Got it for Christmas a few years ago."

Naomi wiggled the toes of her red shoes to catch the boy's eye. "Excuse me if I'm interrupting."

"Why don't we just turn it off," Isobel said, and did it herself on her way to the kitchen.

In the quiet, the boy was left without a voice, without an excuse for his lack of a voice. Naomi felt for her cigarettes in her purse on the sofa, the small rustling, the scratch of the match loud in the silence. "What's the matter? Cat got your tongue?"

He shifted on the hassock.

"Want a cigarette?" She lifted her arm to aim the package at him.

"Don't smoke," he said. "Thanks."

"Maybe you ought to. Want me to teach you?" A tremor crossed her belly, and she felt again the excitement of the cocktail bar, the anonymous man on the stool beside her, just because the room was dim and he was humped in silence. A young lout over there, denied the facts of life by his mama.

Guy sniggered his appreciation of her humor, unsuspecting of the innuendo because he was unaware of her as a woman whom other men took down into their beds.

"No, you sure ain't your father," she mused, defiantly ungrammatical. "He was smaller than you, for one thing. Wiry, nervous, real nice smile. He kept that boy's smile right to the end. I'm not saying you don't have a nice smile yourself, you just don't use it very often. I was telling Guy here," she said to Isobel, returning, "that there wasn't anybody had a nicer smile than Hal. What'd they call it in high school? A winning smile. Yeah, he was always winning."

Isobel settled down with her knitting. "It wasn't just a matter of being lucky," she said. "He worked hard."

Naomi waved it back at her. "Sure, I know he worked hard, but he had a winning streak going all the time. When you get those two things together," holding up two fingers, "you've got dynamite." She winked at Guy. "There was one time he didn't work hard for something he wanted. When he fell in love with your mother, there, she fell right into his arms. Am I right, over there?"

Isobel crossed her ankles. "I guess you're right."

"I remember when you two got together, you and Hal, just kids in college. He brought you home one day to introduce you around. Say, I thought you were mighty cute, with all that nice curly hair. I remember Mama asking you in that just-asking way, asking you what your father did and you said, a grocery store, and Mama said, a market, and you said, no, a grocery store, and Mama said, oh, a little one, and you said, but he's dead now." Naomi laughed, twenty years late an encouraging laugh for the girl.

Guy scratched his back, trapped in the evening that belonged to the visitor.

"You got someplace else you want to go?" she asked him.

"He wants to visit with you," Isobel said.

The sky in the window was dark, the lamplight brighter, the oil heater purring. "Yeah, I remember I thought to myself—Well, here comes that cute girl to Hal's crummy house, old cheap furniture, rag rugs from Woolworth's, his skinny sister with a frizzy cheap permanent in her hair, smiling like a jack-o'-lantern, like a happy loony, everybody living on her file-clerk salary, and Mama asking *her* what kind of people *she* comes from. You remember that, Izzybell?"

Isobel rocked once, and, almost with fear, Naomi saw that the chair was one of those upholstered rockers for matrons. "She was right, you know," Isobel said, her gaze down on her ticking needles and the dragging sock in her lap. "She didn't want him to ruin his chances."

"You know what I said to myself? I said, that little gal's going to be good for him. And I was right."

"I don't know if I was good for him," Isobel said. "But he acted as if I were. He loved his little family, he was a good father and husband, so maybe I *was* good for him. I can't say he was easy to live with, but that's the way it is with ambitious men."

Naomi got up hastily and elbowed her way around the room in search of an ashtray. *Oh, God, what's she doing? Telling a story to a kindergarten class? Who's she talking about? Storybook animals?* "Just because nobody smokes around here . . ."

Isobel was up at once, and came back apologizing, offering the tiny, flowered bowl the guest had used at the kitchen table, and Naomi went on elbowing the room, bowl in one hand, cigarette in the other. "Tell you what," she said, just as Isobel settled into her rocker again. "You go get that brandy. Just a teensy weensy bit, that's all I'll have, I promise. Just to celebrate me being here, how's that?"

Guy brought the brandy, and she took the bottle from him, and the glasses. "Oh, say, this is great! You're sweet." Perched on the sofa arm, she poured the brandy, her wrist perky. "Just a little bitty bit for each. Am I the only one around here who knows how to pour a drink?" *One for the overgrown kid and one for his mother who keeps him a kid.* "Say, this will hit the spot!"

Guy, on the hassock again, held up his glass to

catch the lamplight in the amber brandy, and Naomi watched him focus on the wobbling light, transfixed, herself, by his seeking look, a look she had always observed in young faces and that seemed the essence of their beauty. Maybe she'd had that look herself when she was young, but nobody had ever told her.

"They serve all kinds of great stuff over at Alice Ann's," Guy said. "Her father's got a real wine cellar."

"Take me over there sometime!" she whooped, her humor separating her from the boy just as their antennae were touching. "Hey, listen, you mark my words. Someday you're going to have your own wine cellar and you'll be pulling corks for better men than Mr. Doctor-What's-His-Name. Listen, you don't need a doctor's daughter to get ahead, you've got all you need in yourself. The same way with your father. And maybe your luck'll bring you a wife like Hal's, like your Mom over there. You should've seen them, living in a little house in somebody's backyard, both of them studying away hard as they could. Made me want to cry."

"Naomi helped us out," Isobel said. Her glass stood untouched on the chairside table.

"You make it sound like I was going to sponge off her father," Guy said.

"Listen, you think I can't see you were in love with her, I mean *in love*? It's written all over you."

She took a big swallow of brandy. The warmth spread down into her breasts, a burning bush in both of those silly, leftover things. She saw Isobel take a slow sip and sipped slowly herself, mockingly, thinking how like children they all were, the three of them at a make-believe tea party. "That's the best way to do it," she said, instructively. "You sip it slow. You're right, Izzybell."

"It was a gift," Isobel said. "It must be the best."

Naomi gazed down the length of her legs to the toes of her red shoes. "Say, it's good to get away, believe me. I've got two whole weeks off. I've been in that courthouse seems like two hundred years."

"I've always said that clerks are underpaid," Isobel said. "They do an awful lot of routine work that keeps the wheels going around."

"They do! They do!" her voice big enough to discuss politics with and what was going on in the world. "And even when they get everything microfilmed and automated, they're still going to need clerks. Maybe even more. Less room for the papers and more room for the clerks. How do you like that? So I guess I don't have to worry about a job."

"You get to meet nice people that way," Isobel mused. "You're not isolated. Some clerks are, but at the courthouse you've got all those men who come in to consult the records."

"Most of those guys are married," waving her hand. "And if they aren't, they want the young ones. We had a kid under me, twenty, about the same age I was when I started, but pretty. My trouble was I wasn't pretty to begin with. She didn't work there more than six months and she marries the deputy district attorney. She brings her kids in for me to see, a couple of babies. Real sweet girl." She held up her glass. "Empty. No glass is allowed to go empty around here," she proclaimed, pouring.

"But there must be some nice men who come in . . . ," Isobel persisted.

"You want to know who? Creeps. That's who's interested in *me*. There was a creep came in the other day, some farmer looking up a deed, one of those real skinny guys who've got enormous eyes you wonder what they're so big for. And you know what he says to me? He said, didn't they have your picture in the paper? For what, I said, Queen of the Grape Festival? And he said, six years ago, that time your brother killed himself. He was smiling at me like he thought I wanted to talk about it, like it was what I talked about all the time. Then he asked me where was the best place to eat lunch and I said the Wherry Hotel, and he asked me to eat lunch with him and I said, real cold, that I always brought my lunch in a paper bag. That's the kind of creep you meet on this job."

Silence. This panic, was it like stage fright? Because here she was, Naomi acting Naomi's part, indignantly erect at her desk, withering with her stare the hayseed at the counter.

"What brother was that?" Guy asked.

"Never mind," waving the question away. "Everybody's got to forgive me. It's bad taste to pity yourself."

"Was it Cort?"

"Cort? You crazy? Cort's got the soul of a farm

horse and me, too, and we're both alive and pulling. It's the sensitive ones who leave early. The party's too rough for them."

The silence wasn't broken yet because the silence was Isobel's, who sat with her head bowed, fingers stopped, her feet in fringed moccasins set severely close together. "You are a vile, insane woman," Isobel said.

Naomi hung a cigarette on her lips, searched for matches in the pockets of the borrowed sweater though she knew none were there, found a packet on the sofa, and scratched one across. The flame shook up and down, eluding the cigarette, and, frightened by her own shaking hand, she almost gave up. She leaned back, crossing her legs, blowing out smoke. "That's okay with me," she said.

"What for?" said Guy.

"What for what?" Naomi snapped.

"I mean why."

"Who knows why?" her voice hard and shaky. "Because there he was, Hal O. Costigan, candidate for U.S. Congress, lots of friends, pals, lots of charm. Who the hell knows why? They said he did it because he ruined his chances by running around with a high school girl and they got found out. But who the hell knows why he was running around with her? It's the same question. A man with a nice wife, cute son, why would he want to do anything like that? Maybe he was in love with the girl and couldn't help himself. I guess that's happened before," laughing a high, mocking laugh.

"You stop it!" Isobel cried.

Guy glanced at his mother, but fear of her, like a violent hand laid on him, twisted his head away, forbidding him to see her rage.

Ashes scattered over her lap. "It ain't easy," Naomi said, frantically brushing the ashes away with her left hand, holding the cigarette high in the other.

"I say don't answer me," Isobel hissed. "Just stop it." Since there was no other place for her to go, she settled back into the rocker, tucking her skirt around her, shooting out one leg to see what was on her foot, a shoe or a slipper.

"It ain't easy," Naomi said, a bad student.

"Guy never did anything to you!"

"What do you mean I never did anything to her? What's she done against me?" Unmovable on his hassock, slow to pick up on anything.

Isobel stood up, catching at the knitting falling to the floor. She knelt to pick it up, her back to him. "You didn't have to know about it."

"So now I know!" he shouted. "Is it going to ruin my life?" He had thrown tantrums, Naomi suspected, and he had slammed doors, and he had shouted, but he had never shouted before with this voice.

He was up on his feet, hitching up his trousers, tugging down his sweater. "No dead man is going to ruin my life. A lot of guys I know don't have a father. Do they cry about it? If he killed himself, it's something people do all the time, you're always reading about it in the papers. How's *he* going to ruin my life?" With a palm to each temple he brushed back his hair, shorn too close for the gesture to make a difference. "I guess I'll take the car," he said.

"What for?" Isobel demanded. "Where you going?"

"You asked me so I'll tell you. I'm going to find Lorraine Forbes. You know her, you had her in your class last year. Well, this Lorraine likes me. She more than likes me, she clings to me."

"You leave her alone!" Isobel was following him. "You want to stay in this town forever, a fool, a fool because you got yourself a kid to support?"

"She never leaves *me* alone," he said. At the front door he remembered his jacket. Leaving the door ajar, night air streaming in, he went into the kitchen and came out again, zipping up his leather jacket, striding past Isobel, who was covering her throat with her sweater to keep her dreadful voice from any neighbor passing by.

Guy's footsteps down the path were quick as Isobel's coming toward her. Naomi stood up, covering her face. The fist struck her wrist and, as she lowered her arms to soothe the place, the fist struck her face. But the shock of pain was nothing compared to the shock of Isobel's face. Naomi gripped the weeping woman's arms, forcing them downward, but partway down their resistance vanished, and Isobel clasped her around the waist. Enraptured, Naomi clasped her in return with all the strength of the young woman, years ago, who had been so spontaneously fond of the red-haired, round-faced girl, Hal's bride, little scholar, just learning. In her arms now was the plump teacher body, as spent as her own and to be left by all. Holding each other, they sat down on the sofa.

"Your mother must have felt this way about Hal," Isobel was saying. "She *was* Hal, she lived in him. Like me, what's life got to do with me? A teacher, what's that? What I know I keep back from them. The awful things, the things that happen, I keep back, and pretty soon they're the ones who know. They find out for themselves and they figure I never did."

Isobel was up, searching for something around the room, a note being passed among the students, about her. "I'm glad he knows. I'm glad and I'll tell him more because I'm the only one who knows about Hal. Everybody else thought—well, here's a man who's got respect for himself, who's got it for the next fellow, who's got enough for everybody. You can say they loved him for that in their hicktown way. But he didn't have it, he was faking it. He should have been an actor. It was like a fever, he'd run around with a fever all day and at night he'd come down with the chills. He said someday he'd get rid of himself, he said it was like a mandate. I came down with the disease myself. The neat little Red Cross nurse out in the jungle with her white shoes on."

Naomi was by the window. Beyond the reflection of the room, a watery cluster of lights floated on the night. She covered her face.

"Isobel," she called through her hands, "do you pity him? I'm supposed to pity him, but I've got no pity in me."

Silence. No pity? It was what she had come to hear,

it was what she had come to share so that she wasn't so alone.

"I pity him," Isobel was saying. "Sometimes there's nothing and sometimes there's the pity, and the pity when it comes always makes up for the times I feel nothing. It rushes in where there was nothing."

Naomi heard Isobel catching sharp breaths, heard her go farther away, up the hallway. Alone, she took her hands down from her face. The roof was still over her, the lamp on. Her confession was shaking her heart, her hands, but nothing else was shaken from its harmonious place.

Isobel came back, wiping her eyes on the blanket in her arms. Together they tossed off the sofa cushions, floated down sheets, unfolded the blanket. Naomi had come a thousand miles from the house where her mother had lain, waiting for her to come home from work. She had come all that way to confess about Hal, and it was an affront to her mother that she, Naomi, was given a bed to lie down in. She ought to be wandering the streets of that cold city across the waters.

"I always tried to keep Mama clean," she said. "Her bed clean and everything. Whenever I see a nice clean bed I think of Mama. Even on television, if I see one. My friend Athena has this bed a mile high. Looks like a cloud, lots of eyelet pillows. Her father died just after Mama. She says she deserves a good night's sleep. She got herself this fancy bed."

The overnight case was found, and Naomi held up her black nylon nightie. "Something special, this is.

Got it when I used to go up to Dan's hotel room. He said he liked black lace on a woman, so I got it."

Isobel was kneeling by the heater, turning it off. "That girl," she said, "that girl who Hal . . ."

"Dolores."

"That picture of her, she was lovely, wasn't she? Answer to a prayer or something." She got up, began her search around the room again.

"She came back," Naomi said. "I saw her once. It was on my bus, I was on my way home. She recognized me, too, I could tell. She looks real cheap. At first I thought it wasn't her. She got real thin, and her hair's cut—you remember how it was long?—and you should see the makeup. Before I knew who she was I felt sorry for her, I said to myself, oh, boy, that girl sure thinks she's the cat's pajamas." She took no pleasure now in the girl's change, but she'd taken it then, on the bus, because the change had seemed like punishment, until she admitted what she'd known all along, that the girl warranted none. That bus ride with the girl was the longest ever. There she'd sat, just across the aisle from the girl, clutching her vengeful pleasure to her breast.

Naomi sat down on the sofa and pushed off one pump with the toe of the other. The news she'd brought to Isobel about the girl was a gift like the few others she'd brought. Isobel might be grateful for it, but it wasn't going to last very long.

"Isobel, kiss me goodnight." Lifting her face at the same moment Isobel bent over her, she forced the kiss intended for her hair to come down on her forehead instead.

"Sleep well," said Isobel.

"Don't worry about *me.*"

Naomi, tilting on one hip and then the other, unsnapped her nylons from the garter belt and peeled them down. Barefooted, she crossed the room to turn off the lamp by the rocker, and when she returned to the sofa Isobel was gone. Unzipping her dress, lifting it off, she heard footsteps above her, a secret, surreptitious sound like Isobel's wish that the woman in the dark room below had never come back into her life.

Wrapped in the blanket, Naomi sat on her bed, poured more brandy from the gifty bottle, lifted her feet to the low table, and drank, protected by the blanket as a baby is or a potentate, protected by the brandy against the attempt of the house to expel her, Naomi, who had entered under false pretenses as mute, as deaf, as lacking memory, heart, as a harmless woman climbing up the ramp from the ferry, waving a clean-gloved hand and smiling the ivory-toothed, silver-specked smile of the middle-aged visitor, the past tucked into her overnight case, the past weighing nothing more than the cheap gifts from a drugstore back home, perfume for Isobel and a tie clip for Guy.

The languor from the brandy was spreading all the way down to her feet. She tried to raise her knees, and the languor brought her Dan. "Dan," whispering. She placed a hand each side of him, there at his waist, to form him and to bring him to lie down upon her with the weight of his life, but he denied himself to her and disappeared. Burdened as he was with himself, he could still turn away from those who would further burden him with themselves.

Left alone again, she summoned up the people on the train to be with her. On the train there had been lots of company, sleeping and awake, curled up and sprawling, in all the seats up and down the coach, and she had drowsed side by side with an old woman whose throat noises in sleep accompanied the mechanical noises of the train. The train swept along, wayside lights flickering, vanishing. Lurching figures to and from the toilets, quiet, deformed elderly women—lumping together of breasts and belly, lumping down of ankles—going dimly by in slippers, hardly there and gone, and their quiet husbands in white shirts cross-marked by suspenders, the cross of morning reprisal that the king's scout leaves on the door at night, figures gentle to their own selves as to children who wake in the night and must be led.

Naomi slept, opened her eyes to a lighted station deep in night, the train stock-still, waiting. Someone was pottering about in a little office of unshaded light. What station was it? What town?

"Isobel?" swallowing down sleep.

Isobel, moving around in the light from the kitchen doorway, her bathrobe hanging open, the sash trailing. "You never should have come," said Isobel.

"What time is it?" Naomi whispered. Was it time to get up and get dressed and go down to the ferry dock?

"Four."

Ah! Guy and the girl! The couple in the car! Naomi sighed a long, anxious sigh, a favor done for sleepless Isobel, a comprehension of this terrible night and who was to blame for it. She lifted her feet off the table, aware that a scolding for one thing leads to a scolding for another.

Isobel yanked up the trailing sash. "You come and tell me a little thing like you can't find pity for Hal. So you can't, so what? Is it a crime? Maybe it is, but if it's justified why make it into such a big thing? Why come all that way to tell *me* about it? There are so many crimes, who can keep track of which are right and which are wrong?"

Naomi sat with the blanket around her, no longer like a potentate or a child but like an invalid with a little commonplace ailment that she'd exaggerated into a consuming one. What was it, little or big?

"The ferry leaves at six," Isobel was saying. "You get dressed and make yourself some coffee and call a taxi. It's daylight then." She left on the kitchen light for the departing guest to dress by.

Naomi in her blanket heard Isobel climb the stairs, and her love trailed after, her early love for Isobel that she had brought along, hoping it would keep her upright, save her from tottering around. But Naomi's love was nothing to Isobel, was of no account, a nuisance, and so love gave up on Isobel, couldn't find her again, she was nowhere, and Naomi was alone in an empty house.

12

Seagulls again, flying against the wind, their scornful laughing like that of a colony of lunatics on an excursion. She sat by a window, on a wine-varnished bench in the ferry's warm interior, comforted by the constant vibrations of the engines. Only one person was out on deck, a portly man in overcoat and hat, passing her window for the second time in his morning round-and-round of exercise, pushing against the wind. The rest of the commuters were reading fresh newspapers, their face content with the routine of crossing deep waters. Her overnight case lay under the bench, in it her black nylon nightgown, the pink panties she hadn't changed into, the toothbrush she hadn't used. What kind of dead-letter depository received suitcases left by persons jumping overboard if the next of kin wasn't as close as the next of kin sounds? Isobel, what would she do with it? Or Cort, back home? Pauline would give her things to a church rummage, and who would buy her black nylon nightie for twenty-five cents and feel her lover's hand come in under? With her heel, she felt for the case under the bench to assure herself that she was still there, in touch with her possessions.

The cup of coffee she'd drunk in Isobel's kitchen seemed to have rinsed out her stomach. She'd left a dirty cup and a dirty spoon, and after Isobel had washed them and put away the blanket, would everything be the same as before? Maybe Naomi was to be around forever. She had dug up a root from the father's body to plant in the son, that root that was a need for a reason to stay on this earth. Not the reason his mother taught him, nor the ones that seemed to work for others, not even the real solemn reason you got for going to church. A need for a reason that she, Naomi, who thought she was so smart, hadn't even known about. Why did you need a reason to stay among the living? You stayed because you'd been put there. But when Hal took his life, out there among the willows in the night, she'd learned for the first time that some people never find a reason good enough.

The sun was concealed behind a blanket of high, gray clouds, but its light was reflected on the open waters—a cold, glittering patch far out, like a drifting island. No next of kin would fall heir to the overnight case under her heel. She'd keep it herself. She'd stay inside the ferry, with the morning faces around her, in the warm, vibrating air. She'd stay with the women like herself, combed, powdered, their faces adjusted to the day, nightmares and resignation wiped off by the washcloth. She'd return on the train and hand up to the conductor the long, folded ticket. (She had expected the ticket to be small, like a movie ticket.) She'd unlock her door, unpack, and toss the overnight case onto the closet shelf, and maybe in a month or two she'd move out, move into a two-room apartment closer to work, a place with a tiny kitchen, and maybe get herself a cat. But this anticipation of a time that was to be her own stirred up a vast need to love someone, to use up that future time with love for someone, and it came to her, as she said *Mama, Mama,* inside her mouth with her lips closed, that her love for someone, for all of them, had been her reason for living, as futile a reason as it seemed now. This past love for them, among them her brother in his life before his death, absolved her now of her sin of no pity, and, absolved, she felt the pity for him come flooding over her, like all the pity in the world.

Again the man out on the deck appeared, coming up alongside her, facing her way, the wind thrusting him back, his glasses misted, his hands rammed into his overcoat pockets. He passed her, going on toward the bow, and for a moment he was a forbidden sight — a struggling man, his back exposed.

The gray mound of the city was separating itself into angular buildings and on the large ships moored below the city an array of minute objects became huge anchors, smokestacks, cranes, men. On the roofs of the wharf sheds and high on the log pilings, seagulls watched the ferry enter the slip. The passengers were folding up newspapers, tucking papers into their briefcases as the city filled all the windows of the ferry, both sides. Naomi rose with them and went down with the pressing crowd, quickstep into the terminal, passing under the high small lights of the vast echoing waiting room.

GINA BERRIAULT was an American novelist and short story writer. Throughout her life, she published four novels and three short story collections, including the collection *Women in Their Beds*, which won a PEN/Faulkner Award for Fiction and a National Book Critics Circle Award. A grant recipient from the National Endowment for the Arts, Berriault was also a Guggenheim Fellow, the recipient of a Rea Award for the Short Story, a Gold Medal from the Commonwealth Club of California, a Pushcart Prize, and several O'Henry prizes. She died in 1999.